A Bell in the Garden

A Spicetown Mystery

Sheri Richey

For further information, contact the publisher: Amazon Publishing.

The author assumes no responsibility for errors or omissions that are inadvertent or inaccurate. This is a work of fiction and is not intended to reflect actual events or persons.

ISBN: 9781795787635

Cover art by Mariah Sinclair

The Spicetown Mysteries

Romance by Sheri Richey

CHAPTER 1

Cora Mae Bingham pushed the file cabinet drawer shut and yanked on her jacket lapels to straighten her collar. "Amanda? I can't seem to find the Spicer grant file. Do you have it?" Turning around in defeat, she swiveled her desk chair to sit down.

"I'm so sorry, Mayor." Amanda's brow wrinkled. "I know I just had it and I can't find it anywhere. I'm sure it's got to be on my desk somewhere."

Cora kicked off her shoes under her desk and glanced up at her assistant who was half hiding behind her office door. She stifled her urge to roll her eyes and smiled instead. "Why don't you leave early today? I know you have to prepare for your big weekend, and I'll find the file. Don't you worry about it."

"I'm so sorry," Amanda said as the lines in her brow deepened. "I know I'm a mess. Bryan acts like it's just another day. It's not. It's important that things go right, and I want to make it a great grand opening for his new business."

"I know you do, dear, and I'm sure it will go perfectly with you running it." Amanda had a college degree in marketing but had never had the opportunity to use it. Making the most of her boyfriend's grand opening meant everything to her right now.

"Thank you for your confidence in me. Not just for Bryan's opening, but for everything. The job, the assignments you give me, I really do appreciate that you have faith in me."

"You've earned all of it. I would be lost without you, just like the grant file."

Amanda chuckled as she went back to her desk. "I'll find it. It's here somewhere. I know it."

Cora could finally roll her eyes and smiled as the phone on her desk rang.

"Hey, Connie. How are you today?" Conrad Harris, the Spicetown Police Chief, called at the end of the day primarily for one reason.

"Hi, Cora. I'm fine. The reason I called is—"

"You're thinking about dinner?"

"That, but I keep thinking I agreed to do something this weekend, but I have no idea what that was."

"You did. It's Bryan Stotlar's grand opening for the nursery this weekend. Amanda is all aflutter about it."

"That's right. I don't need a tree, but I should probably go."

"They have more than trees, Connie," Cora huffed. "That's kind of the point of the opening. We'll work it out tonight. Are you going to Ole Thyme Italian Restaurant?"

"Yeah, in about an hour."

"I'll see you there."

"Found it!" Amanda charged through Cora's office door just as she said her goodbye and hung up the phone. "Oh, sorry. I didn't know you were on the phone."

Cora reached for the file, waving off Amanda's concerns. "It was just Connie. He's hungry."

"Are you guys coming this weekend?"

"We are. I don't know when exactly, but we will be out there sometime."

"Great," Amanda silently clapped her hands.

"Now, you go on. I've just got a few things to finish up and I'm done for the week. You go get ready for tomorrow."

With clenched fists, Amanda mouthed the words, "Thank you" as she bounced on her toes and scurried from the room.

Sliding her reading glasses up, Cora saw why the file had been hiding from everyone. The papers were all in a folder labeled "grass seed". Tossing her head back to laugh, she hoped once the opening was over Amanda would return to be her trustworthy right-hand assistant, because her thoughts had been somewhere else all week.

Sheri Richey

CHAPTER 2

Peeking in the greenhouse door, Amanda saw Bryan had his hands in dirt again. The opening was advertised to begin at 10:00am and the panic of it all was closing in too fast.

"Bryan," Amanda yelled through the doorway. "The barbecue grill is here."

"Just have Sam set it up over on the edge of the parking lot."

"What are you doing?"

"I've got a few trees I need to put out. It'll just take a minute."

"You don't have time for that now. We're about to open! You should at least have clean hands!"

"It's not like there's a line at the door." Bryan pulled out a large tub holding four small evergreen trees and it scraped across the floor. "I just need to get these out. I did the others yesterday, but it was raining too hard to finish. I'll be right back."

"But…" Bryan patted her back as he walked out

of the greenhouse door carrying the tub of trees unaffected by her anxious huff.

As Bryan walked up the hillside to the acres of Christmas trees, Amanda hurried back to help with the barbecue. It was a beautiful spring day and she was relieved the weather forecast was good. The Spicetown spring had been cold and wet. Although Bryan had been open for business, the big grand opening event had been postponed to wait out the weather.

"Good morning, Sam. Bryan is planting something up on the hill, so you'll have to tell me what to do with this. I've never worked one this big."

"Don't worry about it. I'll start the fire for you and get everything going. I'm in no hurry."

"Oh, thank you. I have a million things to do and... Well, hello Mavis." Amanda held out her hands as Mavis Bell jogged up panting from exertion. She reached out to take the box from Mavis' arms.

"Hi, Mandy. I just brought some treats over for your guests today. I know Bryan loves my biscotti and I thought you might have coffee set up so this would go nicely with it."

"That's so sweet, Mavis. Bryan is up on the hill, but he'll be right back."

"I didn't know you were planning to cook. This is great," Mavis said tapping the drum of the barbecue grill. "Hi, Sam."

"Hey, Mavis. How are you?" Sam moved around

the grill and grabbed a biscotto just as Amanda turned to take them to the table where the coffee urn was all set up.

"I'll be right back," Amanda called as she ran in the house to search for a serving platter to put them on.

"Amanda," Bryan yelled through the screen of the kitchen door. "Are you in here?"

"In here," she called back as she stretched up on her toes to pull down a large platter from the top cabinet.

"Here. Let me." Bryan pulled out the platter and handed it to Amanda. "I was up there digging and—"

"Mavis Bell next door brought you some biscotti," Amanda said in a sing-song voice, "your favorite. I'm just getting something to put them on and Sam said he would stay and set up the—"

"Amanda, I was digging up there and I hit something." Bryan looked down at his dirt covered hands and shuffled his feet.

"Well, you can finish that later. I need you to move that long table from the greenhouse out to the front so I can set the plants up on it and—"

"Amanda." Bryan reached out for her arms and turned her to face him. "I found something up there."

"Found something? Found what?"

"Shhh," Bryan put his finger over her lips and glanced at the screen door. "Bones."

"Bones? What kind of bones?" Amanda

whispered with squinted eyes. "Like an animal?"

"I don't think so." Bryan released her arms and leaned against the kitchen counter with a worried expression.

"Well, what else could it be?"

Staring at each other in silence, they both jumped as Mavis knocked on the screen door.

"Hey, kids. I don't mean to interrupt but if you don't have a platter, I can just run home and get you one. I should have thought of that and brought one myself. I've got several."

"Oh, no Mavis," Amanda grabbed the platter and raised her finger to Bryan that she would return quickly. "I've got one right here. This should work fine."

"Well, here. Let me set this up for you. I know you have lots of other things to do."

Handing the platter to Mavis, she pulled the screen door shut and thanked her before turning back to Bryan.

"They have to be from an animal. What else…," Amanda said in a raspy whisper. "Are you sure?"

"Well, no. I'm not sure, but they're big, long." Holding his hands out to demonstrate and dropping his arms he searched the ceiling for an answer. "I think I need to tell someone."

"Maybe it's a horse! Your dad used to have horses out here and he might have had to bury one back before the Christmas trees were planted up there. You're just finding it now."

"No, I mean, horses have big bones, but this

isn't a horse. I think I need to tell someone."

"The grand opening is starting any minute. You can't deal with this now." Amanda was determined to make this event special. She had worked on it for months and nothing was going to ruin it. "What did you do with them?"

"Nothing. I left them right where they were. I didn't want to mess anything up, but—"

"We're going to have people showing up here any minute."

"I know, but--"

"But nothing. They must have been there for a long time already. Another day won't matter. I need for you to focus on today."

"Mandy," Mavis called through the kitchen screen door. "Can I start the coffee for you?"

"Oh, Mavis," Amanda patted Bryan's crossed arms with a knowing nod and turned to open the screen door. "I don't want to put you to work. I'm coming. I'll do it."

Amanda pushed through the screen door and across the parking lot with Mavis at her elbow. Glancing over her shoulder, she saw Bryan looking at her through the screen and motioned for him to come outside.

"Mavis, I do have something I'd love to put you in charge of," Amanda said with an apprehensive smile.

"Certainly, honey. I'm happy to help any way I can."

"I have this list. Now I know we can't make

people sign up, but I was hoping to gather some email addresses. You know everybody so maybe you could chat them up and get them to sign up for a sales newsletter?"

"What a great idea," Mavis said throwing her hands up in the air. "I'd love to do that. I want to be the first name on there." Mavis took the clipboard and pen from Amanda to add her information on the top line. "You're such a smart girl. I know that's why you get to work with the mayor. Is Cora coming today?"

"I hope so," Amanda said shrugging. "She said she would try."

"I haven't talked to Cora since the fall when she had that Thanksgiving parade. I used to see her in the drugstore, but I haven't seen her all winter."

Amanda patted Mavis on the back and thanked her just as she saw a car pull into the driveway. "Oh, I've got to get some plants outside and the table," Amanda said pointing. "I need Bryan to move it."

"Go on. I got this," Mavis said waving Amanda on her way.

Amanda peeked in the kitchen door, but Bryan was no longer in the kitchen. Running to the greenhouse, he wasn't there either. Muttering under her breath, "please don't be digging", she charged through the kitchen yelling his name.

"I'm here. I know you need the table moved. I'm coming."

"What were you doing?" Amanda looked around

him as he came through the living room.

"Just looking something up. Where do you want the table?"

"You were on the *Internet?* Cars are pulling in out there."

"Let's go," Bryan said putting an arm around Amanda's back. "You've really got to relax. This is just another day at the nursery. We might get a few more people here today, but even if no one comes, it will be okay. It's not life or death, honey."

"I want it to be nice," Amanda insisted. "Lots of planning went into this and I want it to go right. I want people to remember this and come back. It's important."

"Okay okay," Bryan said smiling and pulling the door closed behind them. "We'll make it nice."

Sheri Richey

CHAPTER 3

Conrad Harris pulled into Cora Bingham's driveway and saw her opening the side door to run out before he even fully stopped his car.

"Ready, Mayor?" Conrad smiled as she got into the car and fastened her seatbelt, pushing her large purse down in the floorboard by her feet.

"Ready, Chief," Cora said sitting up straight with her hands in her lap.

With a curt nod, Conrad slowly backed down the driveway glancing over his shoulder to see if the street was clear. Cora gasped and grabbed his arm. "No, wait, I forgot the cake."

Conrad sighed to release the wasted adrenalin rush and put the car back into drive. "I didn't know they asked you to bake a cake."

"They didn't. I just needed something to take. I don't know why. I just felt like—"

"Okay. Okay. Go get your cake." Conrad moved the gear to park and settled back in the seat.

Slamming the car door, Cora rushed in the house and Conrad turned up the police radio to check on his staff. The spring had been dismal but today there was finally a ray of sunshine. Good weather usually meant more work for the police department.

Bouncing back into the car seat, Cora looked at him with eyebrows raised. "All ready now," as he began backing down the drive again.

"Everything okay?" Cora pointed to the police radio.

"Yeah, it's all quiet," he said reaching to turn down the volume, "so far".

"I hope everything goes well for the kids today. Amanda has been in a constant stir for weeks about this event. After the delay because of the weather, she has done nothing but plot and plan. Getting that added time just made her plans grow. She even has Sammy out there with his grill cooking food today. I'll be glad when this is over so she can concentrate on city business again."

Conrad grunted approval. "Sam's cooking? Great. That will give me something to do. I don't need anything to plant, but I can always eat."

"Have you been out north of town in the last few weeks?"

"Not out to Bryan's."

"Well, I have only seen pictures, but Bryan got a new sign put up and it looks really good. Rodney Maddox painted it from a picture Amanda gave him of the new logo. It says Stotlar's Nursery and there is a little Christmas tree in his name in place of the letter A. It's brilliant."

"Rodney that works for the city?"

"Yes, he's with the street department working for Jimmy Kole. I didn't even know he could paint. He wasn't an artist in fifth grade when I had him in class."

"An untapped talent," Conrad said smiling. "Kids do change when they grow up sometimes."

"And some don't, unfortunately," Cora said laughing. Her memories were full of every citizen in town frozen in time at age 10 when she had been their fifth grade teacher. She judged everything they did today by what they had been like as a child.

"I see a few cars up ahead," Conrad said as they neared the Stotlar Nursery sign. "I see Sammy is manning the cooker."

"See the sign," Cora said pointing. "It looks like he carved it in wood before he painted it. I'm impressed."

"Yeah, it looks great. I see Amanda running around," Conrad said as he drove into the parking lot. "I don't see Bryan anywhere though."

"He's probably hiding in the greenhouse. I think Amanda has taken over the grand opening. She thinks he isn't taking it seriously, so she's anxious for the both of them."

"Here, let me take the cake." Conrad reached for the container once the car was parked and Cora pulled her bag from the floor.

"Thank you. I see Mavis Bell over there. I

haven't seen her in months." Cora released the seatbelt and tugged her purse across her lap. "She's never in Chervil Drugs when I go in. Does she still work there?"

"As far as I know," Conrad said as he opened the car door.

"Mayor!" Cora's head whipped around, and Amanda trotted across the parking lot to greet her. "Hey, Chief. So glad you guys could come."

"Wouldn't miss it," Conrad said under his breath as he handed the cake to Amanda and waved at Sam. Amanda grabbed Cora's arm and steered her to the snack table and Conrad was relieved no one noticed he didn't follow.

"Hey, Sam. What are you cooking today?" The fire was burning, and Sam was adding wood to move it around evenly across the drum before shutting the lid.

"Chief!" Sam turned and shook Conrad's hand. "I'm cooking whatever they give me."

"Skipped breakfast just to be safe." Conrad patted his protruding stomach and laughed.

"Excuse me gentlemen," Mavis Bell said as she came up behind Conrad hugging a clipboard and smiling.

"Hi, Mavis. How are you?" Conrad said as she thrust the clipboard into his hands.

"I'm just great, Chief. The weather is beautiful, and I get to live next door to the best plant nursery around. I'm so excited for Bryan." Mavis pointed to the line on the list and handed Conrad the pen.

"Can you put your email address right there, Chief? Bryan will want to send you his sales newsletter." Conrad dutifully wrote his name and email address on the line as Mavis paused to watch. "You know, his daddy would sure be proud of him if he could see this place today. I sure do miss Bryan's folks. They were wonderful neighbors to have and I know Bryan misses them, too. Sam, I don't think you signed my form." Taking the clipboard from Conrad, she handed it to Sam. "Do you have a garden, Chief?"

"No, I just never had the time."

"Oh, I used to put out a lot of different things, but now I just plant a few flowers and grow some tomatoes. You know gardening is hard work on old knees," Mavis said chuckling and taking her clipboard back while her eyes scanned the customers. "Thank you, boys. I think I've got a few more to catch."

As Mavis hurried off to approach the new customers, Conrad saw Cora working the crowd as if she were running for election again. She always talked to everyone and if there was someone there she didn't know, she would know them before she left. He was content to stand off to the side and watch until Bryan Stotlar caught his eye. Bryan was trying to do the same thing, but Amanda was tugging him around to make him interact with his visitors. Bryan waved to Conrad when he saw him and sneaking away when Amanda was distracted, he headed over to the grill.

"Chief, so glad you could come out," Bryan said shaking his hand. "I really need to talk to you if you don't mind."

"I don't mind at all. What can I help you with?"

Nodding at Sam, Bryan motioned for Conrad to follow him and they walked toward the greenhouse. Instead of going inside though, Bryan kept walking and went around the back corner of the building.

"Sorry, Chief. I know you're off duty and I'm out in the county outside your jurisdiction, but I need some advice."

Conrad frowned as Bryan looked over his shoulder. "What's the trouble, son?"

"I was digging earlier," Bryan said pointing up the hill to the evergreen trees. "I was going to put out a few new trees because I couldn't finish yesterday."

"Okay," Conrad said nodding and glancing up the hill. "Something happen?"

"Well, when I was digging, my shovel hit something, so I hit it a few times with my shovel hoping to break it up. I thought maybe it was rocks or roots," Bryan said wringing his hands and searching for words. "I couldn't break it up, so I reached down and tried to pull it up and it…. Can you come up here? Let me show you."

Bryan scrambled up the incline and waited for Conrad's labored ascent. Trying to control his breathing, Conrad approached the hole that Bryan stood beside.

"I covered it a little. Let me show you," Bryan said as he picked up the shovel and gingerly worked it under the loose dirt. As he raised the shovel up, the dirt fell away, and he let it roll off to the ground.

"Looks like a skull," Conrad said calmly as his mind raced to explain it any other way besides human. "It's missing a jaw."

"Yeah," Bryan said heaving deeply and looking to Conrad for direction. "What should I do? I mean it's got to be human, doesn't it? What else could it be?"

"Well, for starters, let me call the county. They'll need to be the ones deciding what happens next."

"Okay," Bryan said sighing again. Conrad pulled out his cell phone and started to hit the contact in his phone to reach the Sheriff's Office. "Oh, they can't come now, though."

"What?" Conrad looked up puzzled and saw Bryan's eyes squinting.

"Amanda will kill me if I mess up this opening. Poor choice of words. Sorry. I mean it will ruin everything she's planned and…."

"I know what you mean, but it wouldn't be right for me to sit on this. You've told me now and I have an obligation to report it. Let me see what I can do. Put it back in the hole and let me make a call."

Conrad ambled down the steep incline, placing each foot carefully, and walked over to the side of the greenhouse to make his call. It was close to noon and he encouraged the county to delay their response a few hours. That was the best he could do. Finding Bryan in the greenhouse explaining the proper care and planting of lilacs to a customer, he waited for him to be free.

"I asked that they wait a few hours before arriving, but I can't promise anything. I'd recommend you warn Amanda, so she doesn't panic when they arrive."

"Thanks, Chief. I know she won't be happy with me, but I'm relieved to have it off my chest." Conrad patted his shoulder and headed back toward the grill. He could smell the meat was cooking and his stomach was waking up. He would need to warn Cora of the development as well.

CHAPTER 4

Mavis Bell waved Conrad over when she saw him walk across the parking lot. "Chief. I've got you a sandwich right here. It's got your name on it." Mavis giggled and handed the tongs back to Sam.

"Are you working the grill now too, Mavis? Maybe you need to get a bite to eat and take a break." Conrad took the plate she offered him and sat in a lawn chair.

"Oh, it's not work for me. I enjoy helping the kids out. Mine have all moved out now and I miss all the drama," she said with air quotes, "that young people bring."

"I've got enough of my own drama, Mavis." Conrad smiled and took a bite of his burger.

"Well, with Bryan losing his folks, I just kind of try to keep an eye on him. I want to be here for him if he needs anything." Mavis pulled another lawn chair over and sat down beside Conrad with a plate on her lap.

"So, where are your kids now?"

"Oh, Daniel is living in Paxton. He has a job over there now, so it didn't make sense for him to drive. He got his own place."

"You have a daughter, too. Don't you?"

"Yes, Leanne. She's talking about moving back soon with the kids. She has two little girls. Oh, I would just love to have my grandkids here."

Conrad nodded as he saw Cora approaching.

"Found the food, didn't you?" Cora said as she smiled.

"I've got one for you right here, Mayor," Sam said holding up a plate.

"Here, Cora Mae. You take my seat. I see some new people. I don't want to miss anybody," Mavis said grabbing her clipboard.

"Amanda picked the right person to be her greeter. Mavis won't miss a soul."

"Yes, she's got quite a knack for that. She didn't even ask me. She told me to put down my email address. I'm not interested in tree sales, but she doesn't care. I did what I was told."

"Connie, it's not trees. I keep telling you it's a nursery now. Bryan has lots of different plants."

"Yeah, plants, trees, it's all the same."

Cora blew out air and rolled her eyes as he shrugged. Glancing over at Sam, Conrad thought he was a safe distance away to speak quietly to Cora and he leaned towards her.

"I will need to hang around here for a few hours

I think." Conrad peered at Cora and looked back over his shoulder to make sure Sam wasn't listening.

Cora leaned in and whispered, "What's going on?"

"I can call the office and get you a ride home if you want."

"What's going on? Has something happened? Are we keeping an eye on someone?" Cora glanced around the crowd milling through the plants and didn't see anyone she didn't know.

"I'll tell you after we eat," Conrad whispered as he saw Amanda approaching. She was relaxed and smiling so he knew Bryan hadn't told her yet.

"Are the burgers good?"

"Excellent," Conrad barked in relief at her cheery mood. "Sam is a chef."

Sam looked over and chuckled at the remark. "Can I get you one, Amanda?"

"Maybe later, Sammy. Thank you so much for doing this. I would never have been able to juggle the grill and the customers."

"My pleasure," Sam said saluting as he opened the grill top to turn the hamburgers over and add some hotdogs.

"So, what can I show you, Chief? We have bushes and grass seed. Does your lawn need fertilizer?"

"Lord, no. That would just make it grow more and I can't keep it cut now."

Amanda laughed and shook her head. "Not a

yard guy, huh?"

"Not at all," Conrad said and rose from his chair with his empty plate. "Here, have a seat. You've been running around all day. Take a rest." Conrad slipped his phone from his pocket when he felt the vibration and excused himself from the ladies to walk toward the empty back side of the parking lot and take his call.

"Chief Harris."

"Chief, this is Sergeant Cantrell. I'm calling to let you know the coroner is on the way and I'll be there shortly to secure the scene."

"Sergeant, did they tell you there is an event going on here? I mean, there are folks around here at a grand opening for a business and they have no idea what's behind the building. I know we all don't need a lot of unnecessary chaos, but when you pull up, that could happen."

"Sorry, Chief. The coroner is already en route. I can try to call her but she's probably almost there. I'm running late because of another call and just wanted to give you a heads up."

"Okay," Conrad said with a sigh as he saw Alice Warner pull into the parking lot in her late model Buick. "I guess I'll see you soon."

Conrad glanced around the crowd to see if Alice had drawn attention. She had been the county coroner for many years, but she didn't live in Spicetown. Some might recognize her, but he hoped they would just think she was shopping. He knew her well enough to know he needed to intercept her before she asked a random customer where the bones were.

Relieved to see her eyes met his with recognition, he smiled and extended his hand as he approached. "Alice, it's good to see you."

"Chief, I hear you've been digging around today, huh?"

"Well, not me, but I took a look and I do think you'll want to see it. We have a complication though."

"Yeah, Cantrell called me and said there was something going on here." Alice's eyes roamed from left to right at all the visitors strolling by with sandwiches and plants. "I guess he didn't think I could figure that out myself."

Conrad smiled at her sarcasm. "I was trying to delay it, at least delay the squad car because, well," Conrad shrugged.

"I know. They can't get any deader," Alice said with a smirk. "We've got about half an hour. Can you take me there without anyone noticing?"

"I think so. Let's head to the greenhouse. It's back behind there and up an incline." Conrad glanced at Alice's feet and saw she had on jeans and sturdy boots. Motioning with a nod of his head, they walked through the crowd.

§

Cora met Conrad's gaze as he led the coroner to the greenhouse and then glanced over at Amanda.

"I see Alice Warner is here." Searching Amanda's face for a reaction, she saw only a quick glance.

"Oh, yes I see her. I just saw Rodney Maddox and his wife, too. Did I tell you Rodney made the new sign?"

"Yes, you did and it's lovely. I never knew he had such talent." This news gave Cora another reason to look around. Rodney was a valuable city employee, but Cora preferred not to see Carmen Maddox. "I think your event has been a great success, dear."

Amanda smiled shyly. "I'm happy with the turnout. It makes all the work seem worthwhile and I think it gives Bryan a good solid start."

"Well, I knew you could do it," Cora said smiling and patting Amanda on the back. Wandering away as Amanda answered a customer's question, Cora headed for the greenhouse. It concerned her that Amanda did not seem to know what was going on, but she wasn't going to wait any longer to find out.

CHAPTER 5

"Cora be careful," Conrad said as he saw Cora starting up the incline.

"How did you get up there?" Cora frowned as Alice peered down at her.

"Ah, come on, Mayor," Alice said smiling down at Cora. "Dig your spurs in and lean into it."

"Here," Conrad said stepping down part of the way and offering his hand to help pull Cora up the steep hill.

"There you go," Alice said patting Cora on the back with a half hug. "How have you been? Haven't seen you in months."

"Couldn't be better," Cora said with heaving breaths between each word. Looking around and fluffing her hair she saw lots of evergreen trees and a hole in the ground. "So, where's the body?"

Conrad pointed at the hole as Alice squatted

back down beside it and opened a bag she had hidden away under her jacket.

"Bryan found bones this morning when he was planting a tree," Conrad said as he watched Alice intently.

"Human bones? He must not have told Amanda because she didn't even react when I mentioned seeing Alice arrive."

"They look like human bones to me, but that's why the expert is here," Conrad said pointing at Alice's back.

"And Amanda knows about the bones." Conrad raised his eyebrow as he leaned toward Cora, "But he probably didn't tell her he talked to me about it."

"Well, no one will even notice we're back here. I'm sure it will be fine." Cora waved her hand glibly as she cocked her head sideways to see around Alice's shoulder.

"Once the Sheriff's Office pulls up, that might change." Conrad looked out over the greenhouse to the parking lot of the nursery. "Alice says we have about half an hour."

"I told them to go have dinner and relax. Bones aren't an active crime scene and the Chief is here. There isn't any hurry and we don't need a big scene," Alice said as she shifted from a squatting position to her knees. "Cantrell is a rational guy. He doesn't want any hoop-la either. We should be fine as long as the Sheriff doesn't get wind of it."

Cora hadn't thought of that, but Sheriff Bobby

Bell did like to put on a show. He would love the idea of a crowd to speak to, but maybe he was out of the office on the weekends.

"Amanda will be devastated if a squad car pulls up and turns this into a circus. Somebody needs to warn her." Cora looked across the plant covered lot but didn't see Amanda. From the high angle though, she couldn't see the area directly in front of the nursery or the food table.

"I know." Conrad shook his head. "I told Bryan what would transpire, and I explained that I had to report it. I suggested he inform Amanda as well, but maybe he hasn't had a chance to get her ear today."

"Nonsense," Cora said with an eye roll. "I'm sure she told him to keep his trap shut until the event was over when he first told her about the bones. Now he spilled it all to you and he's afraid to tell her."

Cora looked over and saw Conrad nod his head. She hadn't told him anything he didn't already know, but he was too guarded to say it. His restraint always made her boldness more obvious.

"So, what do you think, Alice? We got human bones or not?"

"Yes indeed," Alice said standing and brushing dirt from the wet stains on her knees. "You have human bones."

"So, what happens now? What else can you tell?" Cora looked down at the skull peeking up from the hole and scrunched up her nose. The human aspect seemed pretty obvious.

"I can't say anything conclusively, but I think it's an adult male. Once they get the rest of him out of there, they will be able to tell for sure, assuming he's all in there." Alice shrugged and put her tools back in her bag.

"Who are *they*? You're the coroner. Don't you do all that stuff?" Cora felt Conrad's glare and shrugged. Maybe it was a stupid question, but somebody needed to ask it.

"I'll coordinate it, but the State has to be called in. They have the forensic people that can gather all the details. I should be able to get them down here tomorrow to excavate the area. Hopefully, he's all right here."

"It's not a whole body?" Cora peered again in the hole and thought she saw another bone protruding beside the skull.

"Can't say for sure without digging and it has to be removed carefully." Alice looked down the slope and decided a quick jog down might be easier than easing into it. Turning to look up at Conrad, she watched him slowly help Cora down the hill.

"Going down is worse than going up," Cora huffed as soon as she landed next to Alice.

"Let's go find this young man that dug him up. I've got a few questions I need to ask him," Alice said as she turned toward the greenhouse. Cora was still breathing heavily but scurried to keep up. She knew Alice Warner was at least as old as she was, but she certainly got around better. She was a squared off sturdy looking woman with a gruff straight-to-the-point attitude, but Cora had always enjoyed her candor. Every year when the County Commission held budget talk meetings she had to attend in Paxton, she sought out Alice to sit beside and they would have dinner after the meetings. Despite their different work focus, they had much in common.

"I should go find Amanda," Cora said to Conrad. "She needs to be told and you go find Bryan."

"I'll just browse around in the greenhouse," Alice said, turning around the corner of the building.

At Conrad's nod, Cora turned towards the area under the cloth awning. Amanda had been there most of the day because it was attracting the first walk-up traffic and there were tables with decorated small plant arrangements for sale. Many of the pots had been hand-painted by Amanda and she had seen them in photos Amanda brought to work. With Amanda's decorating skill and Bryan's whimsical plant arrangements, they had been a big hit with the shoppers all day. Cora stood aside waiting for Amanda to finish a sale and then moved up beside her.

"Do you have a minute that I could speak with you?" Cora said in a low voice.

"Sure," Amanda said turning to her.

"Privately?" Cora whispered.

Frowning with concern, Amanda touched her

arm as she looked over the room. "Let me tell Laura I'm stepping away and then we can go in the kitchen." Cora waited as Amanda talked to Laura, another of her city clerks who was helping Amanda out for the day, and then they turned to walk to Bryan's house, pausing twice to greet people they each knew. Cora thought about all the many familiar faces she had seen today and marveled at how well Amanda had drawn half the town out to see a plant nursery. It was spring and that did inspire people to plant and work in their yards, feeling the relief of a hard winter passing. But Amanda had still managed to reach all the town's people with news of this new business and get them all in their cars to drive out. She was really a marvel at marketing. Perhaps her talents were wasted working for the mayor's office, but Cora was going to take full advantage of her talents for as long as she could.

"Would you like something to drink? I've got lemonade," Amanda said as she pulled out a kitchen chair. "Have a seat."

"No, thank you, but I just wanted a chance to talk to you a minute, so you had some time to prepare a bit."

"Prepare for what?"

"Well, you know about those bones," Cora said, peering at Amanda for her reaction.

"Oh, yeah. The ones Bryan dug up this morning? I'm sure it's an animal or something. His dad had lots of animals on the farm over the years."

"No honey," Cora said, realizing then that Amanda really didn't know. "Did you go up there when he found them?"

"No, but he told me about them just before we opened. I don't think he knows really what they are, but I told him there wasn't time for that today. Did he tell you about them?"

"Amanda, I've been up there and those aren't animal bones." Cora waited for a reaction and saw thoughts processing behind blank eyes. "The Sheriff's office is going to send someone here very soon. The State is going to come in and dig the site up and take the bones somewhere so they can work on identifying them. It's a person and Bryan was right to be concerned."

Cora didn't want Amanda to be angry with Bryan. She could sympathize with Amanda's dilemma and she might have delayed the reporting herself, but Bryan had done the right thing. He did what he could live with and what he felt was right. That was what mattered. Now Cora needed to help her do damage control.

"Now? Today?"

"Don't worry, honey. We're going to get through this. They could be here any minute and we just need to meet them in the parking lot, take them around the greenhouse up the hill and try to keep their profile low. If it's just the officer Conrad spoke with, he knows what's going on and he wants to keep it quiet, too. He's not roaring in with sirens or anything like that."

"But what if it's not just him? People are going to ask and what am I supposed to tell them?"

"I think as long as the Sheriff doesn't come himself, it will be fine. We can just tell people the deputies were looking for Conrad and they'll still wonder what happened, but they'll never think it happened here." Cora reached across the table and patted Amanda's forearm. "I just didn't want you to be surprised."

"What if Sheriff Bell comes?"

Cora just shook her head. Amanda already knew enough about the sheriff to know no one could predict how he might react. "No need to worry about something that hasn't happened. The one thing we know for sure is a squad car will be pulling up any minute, so let's get out there."

Amanda nodded and rose from the table. With Cora on her heels, they headed for the parking lot.

CHAPTER 6

"Son, did you touch them?" Alice showed a little impatience in her bark, and Conrad stepped back into the kitchen hoping his presence would put Bryan at ease. He had been stammering around the questions, clearly intimidated by Alice's brisk nature and matter-of-fact style of cutting to the chase when she asked questions. Bryan was afraid of giving the wrong answer.

"No, I told the Chief," Bryan looked up at Conrad with pleading eyes. "I used a shovel and I just pulled it up in the shovel, but I never touched it."

"Okay, so you scooped it up. Then what?" Alice was writing quickly in a notepad even though Bryan wasn't speaking. Conrad peeked over her shoulder but couldn't discern a single word on the page. It looked like a foreign language.

"Once I saw what it was, I mean I thought it looked like a human skull, so I dropped it and covered it back up with dirt."

"Then you called Chief Harris?"

"Well, no. I came inside and talked to my girlfriend, Amanda. I told her."

"Then you called Chief Harris?"

"No. She told me it had to wait until the open house thing was over," Bryan shrugged. "I was going to call, but I'm not in the city limits of Spicetown."

"But you were going to call him? Not the Sheriff's Office?"

"I mean I was going to call the police, whoever, I wouldn't have bothered the Chief directly. I would have called..."

"Bryan told me as soon as I arrived today. It was before noon and he pulled me aside as soon as he saw me. We went up the hill and he showed me the area. We didn't touch anything, and I called the County." Conrad saw relief in Bryan's eyes that Conrad had taken some explanation away.

"Okay," Alice said glancing up at Conrad who was off to the side leaning against the kitchen counter. "So how long have you lived here, Bryan?"

Bryan's gaze shifted to the ceiling. "I'm twenty-eight and we moved here when I was thirteen, no maybe fourteen," Bryan replied, clearly struggling with the challenge of either memory or math.

"So about fourteen years," Alice said pointedly and waited for Bryan to nod in agreement.

"Who lived here before you?"

"Oh, wow. I don't know," Bryan said as his eyes darted all around the room. "Maybe I could find out. My folks, maybe that's in some paperwork they left. I don't know."

"So, did you and your parents move in here about fourteen years ago?"

"Yes," Bryan said confidently.

"You have siblings? Brother? Sisters? Anybody else here?"

"No, just me," Bryan looked over at Conrad again nervously seeking assurance.

"Where are your folks now?"

"They are both dead."

Conrad saw Alice blow out her last breath and tried to ease her frustrations at Bryan's limited answers. "His dad, Larry Stotlar, died 3 years ago and his mother, Stella, died almost 6 years ago. Both from cancer."

"Yeah, they are buried and everything," Bryan said with alarm creasing his forehead.

"It's okay, Bryan," Conrad soothed. "Nobody thinks those bones belong to your parents. They have to be much older."

In an attempt to determine who might have

knowledge of the property and how to contact them, Conrad knew Alice had made Bryan fear he was being interrogated.

"I'm just gathering facts, son," Alice said with a forced smile. "I'm not looking for somebody to blame. I have to turn this all over to the State and they will be asking me these questions."

"The State?"

"Explain it to him, Chief," Alice said as she stood up and picked up her notepad. "I've got to make a call."

§

Cora glanced over and saw Amanda waving her arms frantically in the air, so she hurriedly crossed the parking lot. The deputy was parking at the furthest point from the nursery at the end of a row of cars and they both moved to intercept him.

"Officer," Cora said as she extended her hand when the uniformed deputy closed his car door. "I'm Cora Mae Bingham, the mayor of Spicetown, and this is my assistant, Amanda Morgan."

The deputy smiled and tipped his hat. "Nice to meet you both. I'm Sergeant Cantrell. I'm just here to speak with your Chief Harris. I understand he's here somewhere."

"Yes, a pleasure," Cora said nodding her head. "We know you are here about the bones and we're going to take you to the Chief. He and the coroner are in the house. We just thought we'd try to lead you around the side."

"Ah, okay. You lead. I'll follow."

"I'm going back to the tent," Amanda said to Cora. "I'll be there after I check on Laura."

"Okay, dear," Cora said to Amanda and then reached for Sergeant Cantrell's arm. "It's right this way." Cora led him through the grass toward the back of the property and out of sight to the visitors. The ground was rough and rutted in places, but Sergeant Cantrell seemed very at ease. Cora didn't sense any signs of urgency in him at all. She could hear Conrad's voice as they approached the side kitchen door.

"This house belongs to Bryan Stotlar. He's the one that found the bones this morning when he was digging. He runs the nursery," Cora explained as they walked. "The coroner has been here, and she has looked at the remains."

"Chief?" Cora opened the screen door and walked in with Sergeant Cantrell behind her. "Sergeant Cantrell is here. I don't think anyone even noticed his arrival."

While Conrad talked with the Sergeant, Cora went into the kitchen to look around for the glasses. Finally finding the correct cupboard, she poured Bryan the lemonade Amanda had offered earlier and sat down at the table with him. He thanked her with a bewildered smile.

"Don't worry about anything, Bryan," Cora said patting his hand. "This will create a little frenzy, but it will all be over, eventually."

"I wish I'd never found them."

"Don't think of it that way. That person up there is someone and they deserve to be found. They need to be identified. It's a good thing you did."

"I don't know," Bryan said rubbing a hand over his face. "Amanda is going to be upset and maybe I should have waited, but when I saw the Chief, I just thought I needed to tell someone. I kind of needed to get it off my chest, you know? It's pretty creepy."

"I understand completely, and you did the right thing. No one outside has even noticed. Your opening has gone very well, and I know Amanda is pleased with the turnout."

"Cora?" Conrad had been in the living room with the Sergeant and the coroner and the grave look on his face conveyed bad news before he even spoke. "The Sheriff is on his way."

Cora groaned. "Let me get back out there."

"Why is the Sheriff coming?" Bryan's eyes squinted as he looked to Conrad first and then Cora.

"Just routine," Conrad said. "I'm sure he just wants to take a look at it."

Standing up and pushing her chair under the table, Cora walked behind him and patted his back. "Nothing to worry about. Amanda and I will handle it."

Pushing out the screen door, Cora headed for the covered area where she hoped to find Amanda available. Bobby Bell was just looking for publicity and fame. The shallowness Conrad had hinted at once the election had been decided had proved to be an underestimation. When Bobby Bell was elected last year, Conrad had shared his concerns with her, but she had initially written them off as sour grapes. The men once worked together and didn't get along well. However, Bobby Bell had demonstrated some serious character flaws during his brief time in office and she now tried to avoid him more than Conrad did. He would not make the circumstances easier.

"Amanda, dear," Cora said as she grasped Amanda's arm. "Can I borrow you again?" Shifting her eyes to the parking lot, she tried to convey her urgency and Amanda quickly waved to Laura that she was needed elsewhere.

"Is everything okay?" Amanda whispered to Cora as they worked their way through the shoppers.

Cora waited to reply until they reached a clearing at the edge of the parking area. "The Sheriff is coming."

"Oh, no," Amanda groaned as she threw her head back.

"Yes," Cora turned to Amanda and stopped. "The only thing I can think to do is try to meet him and urge him to park by the Sergeant's car so we can sneak him around the side. He's probably not going to want to do it, but that's the only chance we have."

Hearing murmurs from the crowd behind her,

Cora looked quickly over her shoulder and saw Sheriff Bell had driven his car right up into the grass to park off the road next to the tent full of customers. He had his arms in the air stretching before slamming his door shut and waving to the on-lookers. Another squad car pulled up beside him.

"Good grief," Cora muttered through clenched teeth. Squeezing Amanda's arm first she bolted into action heading straight for Bobby Bell.

"Sheriff," Cora said extending her hand.

"Hello, Mayor. What brings you out here today?"

"Well, as you can see," Cora said grandly motioning towards the visitors, "this is a grand opening for a new expanded business. The townspeople are showing their support."

"I see that," Bobby said with a fake smile.

"I'm sure you are probably looking for the Chief, aren't you? I'm happy to escort you right to him. He's expecting you." Cora cringed slightly but looped her arm through the crook of his elbow and began to pull him towards the house smiling at everyone looking their way.

"Okay," Bobby grunted, appearing disappointed he was going to miss an opportunity to give a speech to everyone.

Once the crowd thinned closer to the house, Cora loosened her grip but kept her voice low. "We are trying not to ruin the event and start a lot of town gossip. Surely you understand how that would just complicate the situation. We don't even know yet what Bryan found, so I'd prefer you make every effort to keep this matter low key."

Bobby stopped in his tracks forcing Cora to release her hold. "I'm sure you understand, Mayor, this is police business and although small town gossip can be an irritant, we have to follow procedure here."

Cora gave him a campaign smile and then raised one eyebrow. "I'm not implying I wish to impede your procedure. I do however want to limit the grandstanding."

With that, Cora turned and pulled the screen door open directing the sheriff to enter and shutting the door behind the deputy that had been following.

Perhaps another bridge burned, but Cora's tolerance for the Sheriff had worn thin after listening to his derogatory remarks at the County Commission meetings the last few months. He seemed to take every opportunity he found to insult Spicetown. Bobby Bell was just one of those people that put others down to build himself up, but she was beginning to take it a little personally.

Locating Amanda easily this time, she looked behind the table Amanda had been using as a temporary sales counter to see if there was a chair or stool, she could use. Her knees were aching, and she wasn't used to this much standing or walking. "Here, have a seat," Amanda said as she pulled a barstool around to the end of the table. "Are they all in there?" Amanda's eyes shifted to Bryan's house.

"Yes," Cora said with a sigh of relief as she scooted onto the barstool. "I can't promise he'll stay though." Cora straightened each leg slowly and rubbed her knee caps. "After I rest a bit, I'll go back over there and stand outside the door. That will deter him from wanting to come back out." Cora winked at Amanda and smiled.

"Oh, Mandy, these little pots are so cute. Laura told me you painted them. This is such a nice place you have here." Carmen Maddox gave them her winning celebrity smile and Cora turned her head away.

"Hi, Carmen," Amanda said warmly. "Thanks so much, but this isn't my place. I'm just helping out and it was really fun painting these little pots. Are you ready to check out?"

"Not yet. I know I'm getting this one for my mama. She just loves ladybugs," Carmen said holding up a pot with flowers and ladybugs painted on it. "Rodney is still looking though, so I'll be back."

Amanda waved as Carmen melted back into the crowd.

"It's thinning out," Amanda said as she stepped back to let Laura use the cash register. "We close in an hour and a half, so I don't expect any new people to be arriving. Thank you for helping. I wouldn't have made it without you."

"Oh, don't think a thing about it. I've enjoyed

it," Laura said. Smiling at Cora she added, "Not as much as my day job though."

Cora could only muster a smile as the girls giggled. Her knees seemed to hurt more dangling from the barstool than when she was up running around.

Amanda moved around Cora's barstool and whispered, "Can you tell me what's going to happen next?"

"That's all up to Alice now, the coroner. It's her jurisdiction once she identifies it as human. She is in control, not the sheriff. He only takes over if forensic evidence shows a crime."

"You mean, like murder?" Amanda jumped as the words came out and she glanced around to see if anyone had heard her.

Cora just nodded.

"Oh, my goodness. I just thought he'd found a horse or something. When he told me this morning, I just figured it was nothing."

"You didn't see it, did you?"

"No," Amanda said squinting her eyes. "Should I?"

"No," Cora said shaking her head vigorously. "I just meant if you had seen it, you would have known. I mean it's clearly…"

"Oh, I feel bad now," Amanda said with a heavy sigh. "Bryan was upset about it and I just pushed it aside and told him we needed to get busy setting up for today."

"Well, he did the right thing," Cora said happy

to see Amanda wasn't angry. "He's required to report it under State law, but I'm sure when he saw Connie, he just wanted to get it off his chest."

"Yes, and then he didn't tell me he did because he probably thought I wouldn't understand." Amanda looked down at her feet and back at the house. "I feel like I should be there, but I can't leave Laura on her own."

"There's too many people in there now," Cora said thinking the Sheriff could leave and improve the atmosphere. Several months ago, Bryan had been questioned by the Sheriff and it had not been a pleasant experience for him. "Connie will make sure they treat Bryan right."

"Here he comes," Amanda nudged Cora as she sounded the alert.

"Hi, Sheriff," Carmen Maddox yelled out waving her hand in the air as Cora rolled her eyes. The Sheriff returned a campaign wave without clearly any specific target. They watched as he returned to his squad car and pulled out alone. The deputy that had been his shadow upon arrival, was not following.

"Here, Mandy," Carmen said as she sat a small potted bush on the table with her little potted plant. "I'm ready to check out now." Amanda ducked behind Cora and went quickly to the task of ringing up the purchases.

"So, what's with all the law enforcement?" Carmen spoke in a hushed voice but even with an effort she couldn't be quiet, and several heads turned towards Amanda for an answer.

"Oh, the Chief's over there," Amanda said with an innocuous wave. "Everybody's looking for him today."

"Well, we always support the blue," Carmen squealed. "Don't we, Rodney?" Carmen grabbed her husband's arm and pulled him closer.

"Hello, Mayor," Rodney Maddox said shyly with a small nod.

"Hello, Rodney." Cora returned his greeting warmly. "The sign is lovely. Amanda told me you made it and I never knew you could do such beautiful work. Maybe we have you in the wrong city department?" Cora laughed at her own joke when she saw Rodney straighten his back and smile. She always felt sorry for Rodney Maddox, but never more so than when she learned he had married Carmen Gentry. He had been a shy lonely fifth-grader everyone pushed around when he was in her class and he didn't appear to have outgrown that yet. "Can you tell me how you did it?"

Rodney moved closer to Cora as his wife finished her purchase with Amanda. "Well, it's really not artistic or anything," Rodney said looking down at his feet. "I just got the picture from Amanda and traced it on wood. Then I took a saw and trimmed it out."

"Well, Amanda didn't give you a picture that was ten feet wide, did she?"

Rodney chuckled. "No, but I just copied it. Then the painting was just like filling in a coloring book.

Anybody could have done it."

"Well, I can tell you one thing," Cora said defiantly. "*This* anybody couldn't have done it and I'd wager a bet most people couldn't." Cora reached out and patted his shoulder. "Just copying the design the way you did is quite a feat. Do you draw?"

"Some," Rodney mused. "Doodles, mostly."

"What about people?" Cora said squinting to peer closely at Rodney's reaction. "Do you draw people? I mean faces, bodies, like that?"

When Rodney furrowed his forehead and paused, Carmen jumped in. "Tell the Mayor," Carmen said as she elbowed him. "Yes, he draws everything. Me standing in the kitchen, the cat, the dog, the tree in the yard. He draws all the time."

"Well, yes, but it's just a pastime. They're not any good." Carmen huffed and walked away, but Cora reached out and touched Rodney's forearm before he could follow her.

"Come see me sometime next week, whenever you can stop in the office. There may be something you can help me out with."

"Sure thing, Mayor. I'd be happy to," Rodney said as he waved and followed his wife.

CHAPTER 7

Conrad blew air out through pursed lips at finding relief in the driver's seat of his car. The lumbar support was a blessing. "So, are you tired? Too tired for dinner? I'm hungry."

"Oh," Cora moaned. "I'm too old for all this. My knees are killing me from all the walking and now my backside hurts from sitting on that little stool."

The sun was going down as they backed out of the parking space and waved at Amanda. The sheriff's department car was still parked on the grass, but Sergeant Cantrell had left for the day, so the parking lot was empty.

"So, I should take you home?"

"No, let's go to Ole Thyme Italian. They have those big padded booths. I'm hungry, too," Cora said as she massaged her knees. "So, tell me what happened after I left you with Bobby."

"Well, he seemed a little put out when he came through the door," Conrad said glancing over at

Cora with a mischievous smile. "Did you have anything to do with that?"

"Hey, I gave him a Spicetown special escort right to Bryan's door as soon as he tried to grandstand by pulling his car up in the yard. I even smiled sweetly when he tried to lecture me on police procedure."

Conrad chuckled. "I suspected as much."

"He thinks I'm an idiot," Cora said scowling. "Does he treat everybody like that or is it just me?" Conrad knew that was a rhetorical question and remained quiet so Cora could vent. "Maybe it's because I'm a woman? Or not law enforcement? Or maybe it's just because he's a jerk." Conrad smirked in response. He enjoyed having someone share his viewpoint without him even speaking it. He had been careful to let Cora make up her own mind about the new sheriff and tried not to taint her opinions.

"Was there much talk out there? Did you hear anybody asking questions about him showing up?"

"Only that woman, Rodney's wife, Carmen. Carmen Macedo I always call her, but she was married to Andrew Gentry and now she's married to Rodney Maddox. She's a nosy one. She asked, but Amanda took care of it."

Conrad only smiled at Cora's crankiness. She always got persnickety when she was tired. "We've run into her before and I know you don't especially care for her."

"Nope," Cora said leaning back and slapping her

hands on her thighs. "She's a man-eater and she's not discreet about it. Flirts with everybody and I know she was cheating on Andrew when they were married. Probably cheating on poor Rodney, too. I've never had any use for her." Conrad remembered being warned about Carmen by Cora's late husband, Bing, when he first hired him. He thought Carmen would try to move in on someone new to town and Conrad had kept his distance. He thought at the time Bing was speaking from experience and suspected Carmen had made moves on Bing, too.

"I think she was Gentry when I first moved to town, but the marriage had ended." Conrad had been aware of the rumors circulating town that Carmen had a baby that wasn't Andrew's child.

"Yeah, she was having an affair with Howard Bell and everybody thinks it's his child, including Andrew," Cora said pointing Conrad to a vacant parking spot she had spied as they pulled into the restaurant parking lot. "That's pretty much what ended that marriage and the talk was all over town. Although it wouldn't surprise me if there weren't several other potential candidates to call daddy. Carmen got around."

Locking up the car, Conrad walked around and up the steps to the entrance of the restaurant and waited for Cora as she trudged up the handicap ramp. Her steps were slower than usual, and he noticed an occasional wince.

Joanne Biglioni, the owner's daughter, greeted

them warmly at the door and led them to their regular booth with promises to be back for their order as soon as she had their drinks.

"So," Conrad said, wondering about some of the things Cora had said during the drive. "You were saying everyone thought Carmen's baby belonged to Howard Bell? Is that the man that Mavis used to be married to?"

"She still is as far as I know. He's just not around anymore. I don't think they got divorced or anything. He just left. It wouldn't surprise me if Mavis threw him out because of Carmen, but I think he was gone by the time she had the baby."

"Howard Bell?" Joanne said as she sat the drinks on the table.

"Yes," Cora said smiling. "We saw Mavis today and Conrad was asking about her husband."

"Mavis is a sweetheart." Joanne pulled her order pad and pen from her apron. "What can I get you?"

"Baked lasagna for me," Cora said and looked to Conrad.

"That sounds good. I'll have the same."

"Coming right up," Joanne said clicking the end of her pen. "You know, I saw Mavis' daughter in here last week. I hadn't seen her in a long time, but she must have been visiting her mom. She's lost a lot of weight I noticed but she looked good."

"I saw her at Christmas," Cora said smiling. "I think Mavis kept her kids during some of Christmas break. I'm sure Mavis would love to have her move back."

"Let me put your orders in." Joanne nodded as she walked away.

"I talked to Mavis a bit today and she sounded like her daughter is considering moving back or she is trying to talk her into it," Conrad said.

"I had heard Leanne was separated or divorcing, but she has two or three kids."

"Two girls I believe," Conrad said as he pulled the napkin from his silverware.

"Speaking of that, I think her son might have been there today. I saw a young man talking to her when I was in the house. They both took off as soon as Bobby got out of the car," Conrad said. Conrad had been looking out of the kitchen window when the sheriff's cars pulled up and Mavis was close to the house at the time. He had wondered why they both looked at the sheriff and left, but Mavis put the clipboard she had been working with all day on the table as they had turned to leave, walking through the grass field that separated her house from Bryan's. The timing could have been a coincidence, but he preferred to think Sheriff Bell caused it.

"Well, if she's ever met the sheriff, that would explain it," Cora said huffing as Conrad laughed. "Is Bryan okay? I mean did he hold up okay after Bobby arrived? He seemed pretty frazzled when I was there."

"Oh, yeah, he's fine. He's a little shaken up, but Bobby didn't even talk to him. He gave him one long look and then went into the other room to talk to Alice. He barely spoke to me."

"A small blessing."

"Alice doesn't cut him any slack," Conrad said shaking his head. He had heard some of their conversation which was mostly Alice telling Bobby his purpose was purely to guard and protect her bones and nothing more. "She told him this was her jurisdiction, not his. She's running the show right now and he can't bulldoze her."

"Good," Cora said as she pulled her napkin from under her silverware and spread it across her lap when she saw Joanne approaching with their plates.

They ate in silence, but Conrad's thoughts were searching for memories of Spicetown when he had first arrived almost fourteen years ago. Cora's husband, George Bingham, who everyone called Bing, had been mayor for many years and Bing had hired Conrad as Spicetown Police Chief. Because he was new to town, Bing had introduced him around and told him countless stories about the town's history and its people. He had filed these stories away in his memories and was trying to resurrect them while he finished his meal until Cora roused him back to the present.

"So, what does Alice think? Did she tell you anything?"

"She can't say anything for sure. It's all speculation, but she thinks it's an adult male. They really hope the rest of the body is there so they can have a better chance to uncover some details to help identify him."

"How long does she think he's been there?"

"She didn't say," Conrad said pushing his plate away. "Based on the questions she asked Bryan, she must be looking back to a time before he moved in there."

"Did Bryan say who his folks bought the house from?"

"He didn't know."

"Well, that's easy enough to find out. They just have to check the county records," Cora said sliding her plate to the side. "You know, I bet Mavis knows. She's lived there a long time."

"I'm sure they'll look into that if they need to. First, they have to get it all moved out so the State can figure out what they've got. Alice said they could be there as early as tomorrow, no later than Monday."

"I hope it's done quickly," Cora said as she picked up her check.

"It's not a fast process," Conrad said picking up his check as he saw Cora scoot across the booth seat to stand. "They bring a team in and remove it very carefully, so it doesn't get damaged."

"Ugh," Cora said. "Amanda will go crazy if this process drags on. I thought with the opening being over I would finally have her attention back on *my* work." Cora turned to sign her name to her credit card receipt and smiled. "I'm sure I'll hear about it Monday."

CHAPTER 8

After a restful Sunday at home, Cora was ready to get back to work on her pet project. Learning she had an employee with natural artistic abilities had sent her imagination into high gear. She anxiously awaited a visit from Rodney Maddox.

"Morning, dear," Cora said breezing through the door. Seeing Amanda on her cell phone, she whispered, "Sorry" before entering her office. Putting her coat and purse away, she could hear Amanda's agitation before ending her call.

"If you don't, I will," Amanda said tersely. "I've got to go. The Mayor's here now. I'll talk to you later."

Twirling the wands to open all the venetian blinds, Cora pushed the button to start her computer and pulled out her chair.

"I'm sorry about that," Amanda said appearing in Cora's doorway.

"Don't be," Cora said with a dismissive wave. "I hope everything is okay."

"Well, I'm a little worried and Bryan is losing his mind. You wouldn't believe all the people out there. They started showing up yesterday and he said there's a dozen more today."

"Well," Cora said frowning. "I guess it takes a lot of people. I wouldn't have expected that either. Maybe that means they'll get done faster."

"He's having a fit because they are trampling his plants and wanting to dig up some of his young trees he just planted. He spent years getting those ready to go in the ground and now they are ruining them. He's out of his mind over it."

"I don't blame him. Unless there's some good reason to destroy something, they should be respectful of his property."

"I told him to talk to the Chief. Maybe he could help, but he doesn't want to bother him. I wish they hadn't put it in the paper."

"He won't see it as a bother at all. Would you like me to call him? I'm sure he won't mind checking on things. He may have planned to do that anyway."

"Would you?" Amanda said squeezing her hands into fists. "I was going to if he came by. Bryan said people keep driving by and slowing down to look. It's horrible."

"I'd be happy to," Cora said turning on her desk lamp. "Did Bryan find any paperwork on the sale of his house? They asked him about it, and he said he was going to look in his parent's papers."

"Oh," Amanda said with raised eyebrows. "He

didn't mention it to me. I don't know if he's had time with all the chaos at his house."

"Oh, okay," Cora said shrugging. "I was just curious. Bing would know if he were still here, but I can't remember."

"I'll ask him the next time I talk to him." Amanda headed back to her desk and Cora lifted her phone. When Conrad didn't answer, she hung up before leaving a message.

"I'm going to go grab something to eat, Amanda," Cora yelled out the door as she slipped her arm back into her jacket. "Can I bring you anything?"

"No, thank you."

"I'll be back shortly," Cora said slinging her purse over her shoulder. Conrad was most likely at the bakery at this time of day and although they neither one needed it, no one could resist the Fennel Street Bakery's cinnamon rolls.

§

"Hey," Laura said peeking around Amanda's door. "Is the Mayor gone?"

"Yeah, come on in," Amanda said motioning for her to enter.

"I couldn't believe what I read in the paper yesterday. When did Bryan find the bones?"

"Oh, I know," Amanda said dismissively. "It's no big deal, really. The State will take them all away and see if they can figure out who it is. They're really old, so it must have happened long before Bryan's family bought the property."

"Kinda creepy," Laura said cringing. "I mean, what if someone was murdered or something?"

"It could just be an old family plot."

"Maybe," Laura said unconvincingly. "You know, Mad Max used to live there?"

"Who?"

"Mad Max. Don't you remember him? He was that weird kid, Max something, Pollard, I think. He moved here when we were in third grade. He was a weird little guy, and everyone called him Mad Max."

"He lived in Bryan's house?"

"Yeah," Laura insisted. "His family went to our church and my dad had to take him home after a skate party once. Our moms were friends." Laura shrugged. "I don't know where he is now, and I don't think they lived there long."

"Bryan didn't know who owned the place before his folks. He's been there a long time."

"You might be able to find out online," Laura suggested pointing at Amanda's monitor. "You can see who owns land on there. I don't know if they post the history."

"That's right," Amanda said pulling her keyboard closer and opening a browser window. Laura moved around behind her and peered over her shoulder. Finding the county's property website, she entered Bryan's name.

"Look," Laura said pointing over Amanda's

shoulder. "Who is that?"

"Stanton Bell, LLC," Amanda said and looked up at Laura. "I don't have any idea but look at the date. He owned all that property for years. See, that name is all over the old plat map." Clicking to enlarge the area around Bryan's house, they saw the same name on every square.

"It looks like he owned that whole side of the county back then. I don't know anybody with that name though," Laura said moving back around to the front of Amanda's desk. "I guess the Pollard family must have been renting the house."

"Weird," Amanda mused. "I'll ask Bryan and see if the name sounds familiar to him. If it was an LLC though, the guy probably didn't ever live there. He just owned the property."

"Yeah and we don't even know how long ago it happened."

"True. I don't know how you find old renters. There could have been lots of them over the years. I guess the State can research this better than we can," Amanda said smiling.

"Well, I need to get back to my desk before the Mayor comes in," Laura whispered waving as Amanda's phone vibrated.

§

Finding Conrad sitting at the counter in the Fennel Street Bakery talking to the usual morning crowd that gathered for coffee every day, Cora greeted them all before ordering. Taking her coffee and cinnamon roll to a table, Conrad soon followed.

"Starting the week off right?" Conrad said smiling at the cinnamon roll. "I thought I recalled you had sworn off these."

"It's your fault," Cora scoffed. "I was looking for you and you know I can't resist these buns."

Laughing, Conrad pulled up a chair and put his coffee on the table. "So how is Amanda this morning?"

"That's why I was looking for you," Cora said licking her fingers. "Bryan is having a hard time with all the people there. It sounds like they aren't respecting his property very well and it's his livelihood."

"I would be upset, too," Conrad said as he blew on his coffee to cool it.

"Apparently some people showed up yesterday, but another big group came today. Does it take that many people to excavate?"

"Well, the State works with the university so they are mostly students I would guess."

"Maybe you could ease his anxiety a little. Amanda told him to call you, but he doesn't want to be a bother."

"I'll drive out there," Conrad said nodding. "Maybe I can influence them to take a little care with things. Depends on who is out there."

"You think the Sheriff would be there?"

"I don't know," Conrad said shrugging. He wouldn't get anywhere if he was.

"Unless there's a camera crew, I wouldn't think he would bother showing up." Cora quirked her eyebrows up.

Conrad looked into his coffee cup and huffed. "I can always give Alice a call if I can't get anyone's ear out there."

"I asked Amanda about the prior owners, but she said Bryan hadn't mentioned it. Have you heard anything?"

"Georgia Marks down at the station told me a family named Burris lived out there before the Stotlars bought it. A young couple she said were having their first baby. She met them because she was pregnant with Jason at the time and they were in some class together. What is Jason now? Maybe sixteen? Eighteen? Something like that."

"I knew a Stephen Burris," Cora looked over Conrad's head searching her memory. "He was a big kid, blonde hair. He might be about 35 or 40 now. I don't think he lives here anymore though."

"Well, nothing to worry about until they know how old the bones are," Conrad said as Cora dabbed at her mouth with a napkin.

"I need to get going. I think I need something from the drugstore." Conrad frowned and then saw the twinkle in Cora's eyes. "If Mavis happens to be working, I'll see what she remembers."

"I'll drive out and check on Bryan in a little bit," Conrad said standing to push his chair back under the table. "I bet there are gawkers out there."

"Yes, Amanda mentioned that, too." Conrad just shook his head.

§

Stepping into Chervil's Drugstore, Cora looked around for Mavis but there was no one behind the counter. Strolling down the aisles she found her squatted down stocking the shelves.

"Hi, Mavis. Long time no see," Cora beamed and patted her shoulder as she walked around her.

Standing, Mavis brushed her hands vigorously over her jeans. "Hey there, Cora. Anything I can help you find?"

"No, I'm just looking. I didn't see you leave Saturday. You worked pretty hard all day. Were you worn out when you went home? I know I was," Cora said chuckling.

"Not too bad," Mavis said opening the top of the next box.

"Your knees are not as old as mine," Cora said giggling. "I'm not used to standing all day."

"I was happy to help the kids. I hope this business venture goes well for Bryan. He's a good kid."

"Yes, they make a cute couple. I don't really know Bryan all that well. I had him as a student, but he was a quiet boy. How long have you known him?"

"Oh, several years," Mavis said. "Since his

parents bought the place."

"How long have you lived out there?"

"Since I married Howard," Mavis said squatting back down to shelve the vitamins she had opened. "Almost thirty years ago."

"Do you remember who lived there before the Stotlars? I'm sure Bing would have remembered, but I couldn't recall."

"You heard about the bones," Mavis said glancing up at Cora.

"Well, yes, I knew about them," Cora admitted, realizing Mavis saw her motivation for asking. "That's what made me wonder. I'm sure the bones are decades old though and I couldn't recall anyone there before the Stotlars."

"I don't remember them all either," Mavis shrugged and pulled another box closer. "There were renters in and out. Most people didn't stay more than a year or two."

"That explains why I can't recall, I guess. By the way, I didn't get a chance to tell you your almond biscotti were delicious. If you ever decide to do some catering or sell some of your baked goods, please let me know. I'm a sucker for sweets." Cora scrunched her shoulders up and smiled.

"Thank you," Mavis said and relaxed her shoulders. "Bryan has always been fond of them."

"I need to get back to work," Cora said as she turned to head down the aisle. "Take care, Mavis."

"You, too."

Cora turned the corner and slipped out the door

for the short walk to City Hall. She sensed Mavis had found her questions about her neighbors somewhat irritating, but maybe Mavis had received a lot of inquiries from shoppers today. Spicetown could be a gossipy place but Mavis didn't usually participate. Living next door to the discovery of buried bones and being at the grand opening when they were found had probably put her in a spotlight she didn't relish. Cora regretted adding to her angst, but she texted the information to Conrad as she walked.

§

Breezing through Amanda's office to reach her own, Cora tugged off her coat. "I'm back. Did I miss anything?" Not waiting for an answer from Amanda, she pulled open her desk drawer and dropped her large satchel purse inside before sitting down.

"Actually," Amanda said entering Cora's office right behind her, "I found out who owned Bryan's farm. Well, kind of…"

"That's good," Cora said leaning forward on her elbows. "Who was it?"

"A company called Stanton Bell, LLC. He owned, or it owned almost all the land north of town until about thirty years ago when it started selling off small plots to different people."

"Interesting," Cora said humming. "That name is familiar to me, but I don't know why."

"Well, the company had a Cleveland address. I didn't find any paperwork filed to subdivide it, but it started selling in five-acre lots up to some forty-acre pieces to different people after that. It still owns some undeveloped land out there."

"And how did you find all this out? Did you hear from Bryan?"

"No, I looked it up online. The county recorder's office had some information and then I called them and got the rest."

"Who owns the property next door?"

"Where Mavis lives?"

"Yes," Cora said. "Did you notice when you looked up Bryan?"

"No, but I can check. Wouldn't it be Mavis? I mean she's been there forever."

"Perhaps," Cora said shrugging. "It may have her husband's name on it. I think he was living there before they married."

"Oh, I didn't know him," Amanda turned in the doorway. "Let me check."

"One more thing," Cora said raising her index finger. "Check with the Secretary of State and see what you find out about the LLC. It may only have an attorney's name for whoever filed it, but you never know. I think that's probably online too."

"Oh, good idea," Amanda said nodding and heading back to her desk.

Cora sent Conrad another text asking him to call when he was free so she could share Amanda's information. Something was eating at her and she decided it was time to do her own online searches.

Sheri Richey

CHAPTER 9

"Bryan," Conrad said waving his hand to greet Bryan who was standing at the base of the incline to his tree lot. Amanda had been right. There had to be at least twenty-five people around, most wearing white paper sterile covers over their clothes and shoes.

"Oh, Chief. Am I ever glad to see you," Bryan said shaking his hand. "These people are ruining my trees. Can you talk to them?"

"Well, who is in charge of the site?"

"The coroner has been here most of the morning, but I don't see her right now. That man with the blue hat," Bryan said pointing to an older gentleman with glasses who was standing behind the group in white, "He's from the University. The guy sitting on the side in the yellow shirt, he's from the State. He hasn't done anything much, just stand around."

"Did they tell you how long all this would take?"

"No, they don't want to talk to me at all. In fact, they keep trying to run me off, but I'm not leaving. I've got to keep an eye on these trees. The ones on the side, the little ones, those are Fraser Firs. I just planted them, and they need to be watered. They're not like the other trees. The others are Scotch Pines and they're established. I've spent years growing these trees to a size where I could plant them. I don't want to lose them. They're very fragile right now."

"I'll see if I can get a word with the coroner. See if I can find anything out," Conrad said scanning the area for her gray, almost white, hair. "Is the Sheriff's office here?"

"There's a deputy sitting out in his car, but he's planning to leave. They keep someone here at night, but I guess he doesn't have to stay when everybody else is here. It's been a circus."

Catching a glimpse of Alice's cotton top, Conrad patted Bryan on the arm and started up the incline.

Nodding a greeting to those he passed through, he finally reached Alice.

"Hey, Chief," Alice said cheerily. "What brings you out to our party?"

"It's a beautiful morning," Conrad said smiling. "Just checking in on Bryan. Do you have a minute?"

"Sure thing," Alice said stepping away from the group of students. "I know the young man's worried about his trees, Conrad, so before you say anything, rest assured, we aren't here to hurt anything."

"So, he's talked to you," Conrad said looking around at all the equipment and people on their knees with tools.

"Oh, yes," Alice said shaking her head. "He's done little else."

"But Alice, this is his only source of income and you are threatening that. I can't pretend to understand all this, but I know that these little trees here on this end are fragile and require some care from him. He's just starting out in the nursery business and…" Conrad saw Alice nodding her head robustly with a bored expression. Obviously, Bryan had shared his concerns with her. "How long is this going to take?"

"No idea, Conrad," Alice said shaking her head. "This excavation stuff is not my bag. It'll take as long as it takes to keep the evidence intact. It does look like the whole skeleton is there though and that's a huge advantage. If we can get all the bones out in good shape, we have a real chance at getting ID and maybe even a cause of death."

"Any idea how long the body has been here?"

"That's the hardest thing to determine and we may never know," Alice said glancing at her phone. "I'd say somewhere between ten years and forty years. Maybe we can give you a better guess than that once the bones are cleaned."

"I know most of these are students and this is a

great learning experience for them, but please try to get this removed as quickly as possible," Conrad pleaded. His fear was the university leaders were keen to drag out the operation focusing on the learning opportunity and disregarding Bryan's needs.

"I definitely will," Alice assured him as she placed her hand on his upper arm. "I'm sure he wants to know who this person is as much as we do though, so he needs to understand they will probably take this corner of his field to sift for any surface clues. They are trying not to disturb his little trees, but they'll do whatever they think is necessary. If they find something near a tree, they are going to keep going."

"I'll try to explain that," Conrad said shaking his head.

"He doesn't want to look uncooperative." Alice raised her eyebrows and gazed at Conrad oddly. Had Bryan's fussing been interpreted as him trying to impede the investigation?

"I trust you'll do your best," Conrad said as he turned to step down the hill. Bryan was at the foot of the incline anxiously awaiting his arrival and offered him a hand when his footing slipped near the bottom.

"Let's go inside for a minute," Conrad said to Bryan with a furrowed brow. It was time to lay some things out clearly before Bryan's concerns became a target of investigation.

§

"Hi, Cora," Conrad said through his car's Bluetooth speaker. "I got your message. I'm driving back to town now. I went to see Bryan."

"Oh, good. Is he okay?"

"Yeah, he's fine. He's just really worked up about losing some of those new trees he just planted. They are some kind of special type or something. Amanda was right though. It's a mess out there and way too many people tromping around."

"Was the Sheriff there?"

"No, a deputy was leaving when I got there but they are posting one there at night. Alice was there, a State guy looking on and a bunch of university students. A lot more people than I expected."

"That could be good though," Cora suggested. "Maybe it will be over quickly with that much help."

"I don't think so," Conrad said with regret. "I got the impression they are using this as a teaching moment, and that's dragging it out. I heard the guy in charge of the students talking them through each little step, explaining things and making them do it over. It sounds to me like a bunch of wasting time, but what do I know…"

"Tsk, that's unfortunate. Were you able to convey Bryan's concerns to Alice?"

"Yes, but she was already very aware. Apparently, Bryan has been trying to talk to them all day. He just wasn't feeling like they gave his concerns any merit."

"He's probably right. They have a different motive."

"Exactly," Conrad said as he coasted into town. "So, what did you find out when you went shopping?"

"I was surprised Mavis wasn't very forthcoming. She seemed a little miffed at my questions."

"She seemed really friendly Saturday."

"I know but she let me know right off she knew I was asking because of the bones. Anyway, she did tell me there were renters in and out before the Stotlars. None of them stayed long."

"That will be hard to trace," Conrad said as he pulled into his parking space at the police department.

"Oh, but the reason I asked you to call," Cora said almost forgetting Amanda's information, "the land was owned by Stanton Bell, LLC. Do you know that name?"

"No, it doesn't mean a thing. Do you?"

"I feel like I do, or I should. It sounds so familiar, but I can't place it."

"Stanton Bell? I wonder if it's any of Bobby's family."

"Or Howard's. Mavis moved out there when she

married Howard Bell. Is the sheriff related to Howard?"

"No idea, but it may not even be a person named Stanton Bell. It may be a two people, one named Stanton and the other Bell."

"I hadn't thought of that," Cora mused. "Amanda's checking on the LLC part. Maybe the officers of the company are public."

"I'm at the office now. Let me know," Conrad said as he prepared to turn off the car and they agreed to talk later. Walking into dispatch, there were several officers milling about. The day patrol was usually pretty slow in the mornings.

"Hey, Chief," Officer Roy Asher said between bites of his breakfast burrito. "Heard you found some bones this weekend. Any news on them yet?"

"No, it's the county's case. I just happened to be out at the Stotlar place."

"Yeah, it can't be the Stotlar's doing though," Roy said as he chewed. "They were good people. Bryan, too."

Conrad nodded and took some messages Georgia handed him.

"We got any missing people?" Roy asked. "I mean like from a long time ago. Any missing reports open?"

"Chief's already pulled them," Georgia said smirking.

"I'll take a look but without a time frame, I don't know what good it will do," Conrad said shrugging.

"We could have a murderer right here in

Spicetown," Roy said wadding up the wrapper from his breakfast and attempting to shoot it into the trash.

Conrad picked up the failed attempt and dropped the wrapper into the trash can frowning at Roy. "Let's not jump to conclusions."

"Course not, Chief. I'm just saying…" Roy stood up and pulled on the waistband of his pants which kept sneaking under his belly. "I better get out of here. See you later, Chief."

Conrad waved at Roy and looked down at the messages Georgia had handed him.

"Georgia, do you know what the Sheriff needed?"

"Nope," Georgia said spinning around in her chair to face Conrad. "He didn't say, but it didn't sound urgent."

Nodding, Conrad walked back to his office and started his coffee maker before sitting down at his desk. The other message was one to call Karen Goldman, a Spicetown resident he had helped last summer when her young son wandered too far from home. He hoped that hadn't happened again.

"Karen? This is Chief Harris. I got a message you called."

"Yes. Thank you for calling me back. I really hate to bother you, but the news this weekend has… I just had to say something."

"It's no bother at all. What has you concerned?"

"Before you were hired, my uncle was missing. I heard about those bones and I don't know how long ago they were buried there, but I wanted you to know. He lived right next door to the Stotlar's house, and no one has heard from him in over fifteen years."

"Karen, who is your uncle? Did you file a police report?" Conrad shuffled through the files Georgia had pulled for him.

"His name was Howard Bell," Karen said. "He lived north of town my whole life."

"Bell was your maiden name?"

"No, he's my mom's brother. She filed a police report, but not right away. His wife said he just left, so we thought we'd hear from him. We thought maybe they were having problems."

"I understand. What's your mother's name?"

"Miriam Landry. She's the—"

"Yes, I know Miriam. So, she filed the report? Do you remember the year?"

"I was in high school when he disappeared, so it's been close to twenty years ago, I guess. Uh…"

"I see it," Conrad said pulling a file out. "We have the report. I'll make sure it gets to the Sheriff."

"I thought you were handling it."

"No, I was just on the scene initially. The Stotlar's property is in the county so the Sheriff's Office will handle the case, but don't expect to hear anything soon, now."

"I know. I just wanted to bring it to your attention in case we can help somehow, my mom and me. Because of where it is, you know," Karen stammered and sighed heavily. "It just never made any sense. Uncle Howard wouldn't just disappear and never contact anyone in the family again. He wasn't like that. We've always thought something must have happened to him."

"Is your family related to Sheriff Bell at all?"

"I don't know the Sheriff, but my mom says we are distant cousins or something."

"Well, I'll pass your information on and someone will contact you if they need your help, but Karen, it could be anything up there. They really don't know much yet."

"I understand," Karen said sadly. "I just had to say something."

"I'm glad you did. You take care now and tell that boy of yours not to wander off," Conrad said remembering walking up to the boy who was playing outside several blocks from home one day. He had ridden too far on his bicycle, probably lured by playmates, and lost track of time. Karen had called the PD in a panic.

"Thank you," Karen said laughing. "I think you scared him too much for that to ever happen again."

CHAPTER 10

"Mayor?" Amanda appeared at Cora's office door and Cora looked up over her reading glasses. "Rodney Maddox is here. He said you asked him to stop by?"

"Oh, yes, yes," Cora said pulling her glasses off and standing. "Have him come in. You come in, too, Amanda." Grabbing a notebook and pen, Amanda showed Rodney through the office door and pointed to a chair.

"Hello, Rodney. Thank you for stopping in."

"Happy to," Rodney said dipping his head down and then glancing at the chair Amanda indicated. Rodney sat down gingerly and hunched his shoulders. "How can I help you, Mayor?"

"Well, Rodney, I was so inspired when I looked at the sign you did, and it gave me an idea. I'm hoping you can help me with something, but understand, it is not part of your job. You can say no if you want. If it's something you would like to do though, I will pay you for your work on it. It's separate from your regular city job. Okay?"

"Okay," Rodney said shuffling his feet to cross them at the ankles and then reverse them again.

"Let me explain," Cora said sitting up straight and clasping her hands. "I have plans this summer to honor the man Spicetown was named after. The city received a grant to erect a statue of John Spicer. It is still several months off, but I want to advertise the event."

Rodney nodded as Cora glanced at Amanda with a mischievous smile.

"The City Council did not see fit to finance this unveiling and the grant money does not cover advertisement, but I have a small fund for public announcements and general communications, like newspaper ads and website updates. I plan to use that to get the word out about the event." Cora paused again but when Rodney did not speak, she pulled a folder from a stand on her desk and opened it.

"You see, I have a picture of our founder, John Spicer," she said handing it to Rodney who studied it intently.

"As you can see, it's not very clear. It's an old photo that was colorized and it's very hazy. The edges are deteriorating and discolored." Cora accepted the photo back from Rodney gently. "The statue is not finished yet, so it is the only image I have, and I'd like to use it in our advertising."

Cora raised her eyebrows and nodded. Surely, Rodney could see where she was going, yet he made no indication.

"Rodney, do you think you could draw this picture larger and clearer? Like you did Amanda's logo? I would need it to be at least five inches wide or so. I could give you a copy to take, but I've tried blowing it up on the copy machine and it just isn't clear enough to use in the paper or on ads. I need something crisper. Does that make sense?" Cora leaned forward and slipped her glasses back on.

"Well," Rodney said with a frown. "Can I see that again?" Cora handed it back to him and Amanda offered him a copy from the photocopy machine that she had made earlier. "Yeah, yeah, I think I can do that. You want like a five by seven or so?"

"Yes," Cora said beaming. "Just a pencil sketch is fine or whatever you think best. It will be copied, put on our website and maybe in the newspaper. Does two hundred dollars sound fair?"

"Wow," Rodney said sitting up straight in his chair. "That sounds great. Maybe I can get that Japanese Maple Bryan had out there Saturday if my wife doesn't hear about it. Did you see it? They are really beautiful in the fall. All the leaves are a dark red. I've got a place all picked out for it."

"I didn't know you were a landscaper, too," Cora said smiling.

"Yeah, I love working in the yard. I'm hoping

Bryan gets some landscaping jobs and then maybe I can do some extra work for him," Rodney said smiling. Amanda smiled back and nodded.

"Your wife doesn't like you doing yard work? Most would be happy that their husband tended to those things well."

"Oh, she wants the yard mowed and all, but she does *not* want me to spend money, no two hundred dollars on a tree. She'd rather get clothes or something with it." Rodney shifted in his chair and pulled at the knees of his blue jeans.

"Well, that's probably true of most wives," Cora said smiling politely. "How long have you two been married?"

"Almost ten years."

"Really? Has it been that long?"

"Yeah," Rodney said. "Little Casey is seven now."

"You have a stepson too, right?"

"Yeah, Andy, but he's a senior this year."

"My how time flies," Cora said gazing up at the ceiling. "I didn't remember his name was Andy. He's named after his father, Andrew? I thought I remembered he had an unusual name, something different."

"His real name is Anderson."

"Ah, yes. That's it," Cora said chuckling. "A very grown up name, isn't it? It makes sense now that you call him Andy. Well, do you have any questions? About the drawing, I mean."

"When do you need it?"

"I think by the middle of May we will probably want to start promoting. Is that enough time?"

"Oh, sure. That won't be any problem at all."

"Well, I appreciate it, Rodney, and remember you can always stop in if you have any questions. You know how to reach me or Amanda," Cora said pointing at Amanda.

"Sure thing, Mayor," Rodney said rising from his seat and heading for the door. "No problem at all." With a quick wave, Rodney was gone, and Amanda sat smiling at Cora.

"So, what's up?" Amanda was still grinning with a quizzical tilt of her head.

"Not a thing," Cora said innocently. "I told you I was going to see if he could draw us an ad for the unveiling."

"Yes, but the questions about Carmen..."

"Just small talk, dear," Cora said shuffling her papers on John Spicer back into the folder and filing it away without meeting Amanda's eyes.

"Oh, okay," Amanda said with a searching look as she rose slowly and returned to her desk.

§

Conrad reluctantly returned Sheriff Bell's call after he'd had a cup of coffee and read Miriam Landry's report on her missing brother, Howard Bell.

"Connie," Bobby barked out on the phone once

Conrad's call was transferred to him.

"Sheriff," Conrad replied respectfully. "I got a message you had called."

"I did. I know you got a little tangled up in this Stotlar bone case, but I may need a little something from you, if you can spare the time."

The dance they did with all the formalities was tedious but necessary. Conrad would have preferred to just call him and say, 'Hey, Bobby. What do you want?' That was always the end result. Bobby only contacted him if he needed something from him, but it wouldn't be proper to take shortcuts.

"I'm happy to help. What can I do for you?"

"Well, I was looking through your missing person cases in the database for the last twenty, thirty years and there's one there we might need to develop."

"I was doing the same review. Which case is it that concerns you?"

"In '99 there was a report that Howard Bell was missing. I wouldn't ordinarily be too concerned, but he did live next door to the property in question, so it might require some attention."

"Yes, but there is another in 2001 and an older one in '95. Alice told me she didn't really know how long the bones had been there. Have they found anything to narrow it down?"

"Not to my knowledge, but I've got my team pulling records on every missing report in the county for the last thirty years, at least those that were adult males. Alice seemed pretty sure of that part."

"I've done the same. What has you interested in Howard Bell?"

"I've got some detectives searching for medical and dental records on all of them because the State said this ID would be expedited. I expect them to start asking for info to match against as soon as the bones are cleaned."

"You need me to do the same?"

"Well, yes," Bobby said hesitating slightly. "At least on Howard Bell. They might ask for family DNA if we can't find any medical or dental connections."

"Okay," Conrad said waiting for Bobby to explain his reason. He wasn't going to ask. He wanted Bobby to be forthcoming on his own, but it was another game they played. "Just Howard though?"

"For right now, yes, although the detectives may be reaching out if they need anything from a Spicetown doctor or dentist. I've told them to contact you if they need to."

"Okay, that will be fine."

"You know, with the name the same, I don't want there to be anyone questioning anything. I don't know Howard Bell, but it might look funny."

"I understand," Conrad said smiling at his image of Bobby squirming. "We'll get right on it."

"Great. Talk to you later," Bobby said disconnecting the line before Conrad could tell him goodbye.

Cora Mae was going to love this news. Miriam Landry could fluster Cora quicker than anyone else in town. It was time to take a walk to the Spicetown Chamber of Commerce.

CHAPTER 11

Cora tossed her mail on the hall table as she walked in the house. The hearty aroma of minestrone that had spent the day cooking in her crock pot filled her home. She didn't cook often, but when she did, she cooked big. She always tried to make something on Monday that she could eat as leftovers throughout the week.

Kicking her shoes off, she pulled a bag of peas from the freezer to add to her soup, set a timer for thirty minutes, and went to change into something comfortable. Returning to the kitchen in her sporty track suit she was debating whether cornbread would be a proper side for her meal when her doorbell rang.

"Hi, Sandy," Cora said tilting her head and

smiling. Sandy Nash lived across the street with her husband, Marty. Aside from a casual wave, Cora had never really talked to the couple much since they moved in last summer.

"Oh, Mayor, I hate to bother you," Sandy said placing her hand on her heart. "If you're not too busy, can I talk to you for just a minute?"

"Certainly. Come on in." Cora led her down the hallway. "Please come back in the kitchen. Would you like something to drink?"

"Oh, no. I don't mean to interrupt. I know you just got home. I've been watching for you because I didn't want to trouble you at work."

"You're not interrupting anything and please, call me Cora. Now, what can I do for you?"

"Well, I heard about the bones they found this weekend," Sandy said sitting down in a kitchen chair. "I know they don't know who they belong to, but I think they may be my friend, Dixie's, Dixie Martin."

"I don't think I know her."

"She was my roommate before I married Marty. We lived over on Rosemary Road in a duplex and we both worked together at Sesame Subs. Dixie wasn't from Spicetown though. She lived in Paxton and was driving back and forth every day. I met her at work, and I wanted to move out of my parents' house, so we rented a place together. We became really good friends and she just disappeared one day. No one has ever heard from her again. I'm afraid, I mean I've always thought something bad had to have happened because she wouldn't do that. She would contact me or her mom. She was close to her mom. There was just no explanation."

"When did this happen?" Cora said with concern, pulling a chair out and sitting beside Sandy. "I remember Bing mentioning this to me."

"It was right before Christmas in 1999. I didn't, I didn't report it right away, because…" Sandy swiped tears from her cheeks. "I thought she went away early for Christmas. I thought she would call, but then…"

Cora turned toward Sandy to take her clasped hands in her own.

"Then her mom called, and I lied to her." Sandy gasped as her body shook with sobs and Cora jumped up to get her a tissue.

"It's okay," Cora said. "Let me make you some tea." Cora grabbed the teapot from the stovetop and filled it with water to allow Sandy some time.

"Dixie was dating a married man and it was a secret," Sandy said as Cora sat a ceramic tea bag holder on the table and returned to the counter to get cups.

"Was this man from Spicetown?"

Sandy nodded as she dabbed at her eyes. "Dixie told me he was going to leave his family and be with her on Christmas, so I just thought that's where she was."

"So, you weren't worried at all at first. That's understandable."

"But she didn't call me," Sandy said blowing her

nose. "Boyfriend or not, it wasn't like her not to call me."

"Well, back then we didn't all have cell phones," Cora said. "We weren't as in touch with each other all the time."

"That's true. So, when her mom called looking for her, I kind of felt caught in the middle and I wasn't going to tell her about Howard. It wasn't my place. I just told her I didn't know where she was."

"But that wasn't a lie, Sandy, so you didn't do anything wrong."

"I know," Sandy said sniffing. "But if I'd told somebody sooner, maybe they could have found her."

"Who was this Howard?"

"Howard Bell," Sandy said with a dismissive wave. "He disappeared too, so I just thought they were together. Howard used to come in almost every day for lunch. That's how they met."

"Eventually you told her mom, I guess."

"Yes, I got worried. Well, first I got mad she hadn't called me, had made me worry about her. Then I felt bad for getting mad and I got scared. I was just, I was young. I didn't even know what to think."

"So, her family?"

"Yeah, they kept calling. Her mom kept asking, then her mom came to the restaurant. She wanted to talk to the manager and to me. She was panicking and I told her what I knew."

"Her mom didn't know about Howard Bell?"

"No, and she went straight to the sheriff's office. She made them go to Howard's house to question him, but he wasn't there either."

"Did the deputies talk to you?"

"Yeah, her mom filed a report and they came and talked to me. I never heard anything else. I know they didn't find her."

"Well," Cora said getting up from the table and unplugging her crock pot, so it didn't overcook. "I can tell you that they think the body is an adult male. Nothing for sure yet, but that's what it's looking like."

"But maybe it's Howard and she's there somewhere, too. He lived out that way. Maybe his wife found out and killed them both."

"Now, let's not jump to conclusions here," Cora said coming back to sit beside Sandy again. "You don't want to go around speculating about these things."

"I know," Sandy said shaking her head in remorse. "I shouldn't have said that, but something happened, and Howard lived out on the same road north of town."

"I will make sure the Chief and the Sheriff know about your concerns, Sandy. They probably have access to the report Dixie's mom filed, but I will make sure to let them know about her."

"Thank you, Mayor. That's really all I was hoping for. I don't want her forgotten. I feel so guilty for the way it happened and I've never forgotten her."

"I'm glad you came over."

"I'm going to get out of here so you can have dinner now," Sandy said chuckling. "I'm so sorry to blubber all over you."

"That's quite all right, dear," Cora said patting Sandy on the back as they walked towards the door. "You're welcome any time."

"Thank you, Mayor," Sandy said as she walked out the door and hurried across the street.

Cora walked back to the kitchen and opened the cabinet for the cat food. Marmalade rubbed against her shins as she poured some food in a bowl for her. "So, Howard Bell is a dog," Cora said stroking her hand down Marmalade's orange back. "Poor Mavis."

§

"Chief," Georgia Marks said as she peeked her head in Conrad's office. "Miriam Landry is here to see you."

"Thanks, Georgie. You can send her on back."

Conrad emptied the coffee grounds from his coffeemaker and put in a new filter.

"Miriam, please have a seat. It's good to see you."

"Really, Conrad. I can't believe you asked me down here," Miriam said looking around his office with disgust.

"Well, I've been trying to track you down for three days, Miriam. I've been to the Chamber twice and your house. I can't seem to get you to give me a minute, so short of arresting you, I didn't know what else to do."

"Ah," Miriam huffed. "And what is so important? What exactly do you want from me, Conrad?"

"Would you like some coffee," Conrad asked as he poured water into his coffeemaker and turned it on.

"No," Miriam said tersely. "I have somewhere to be. Let's just get to the point."

"Well," Conrad said spinning his chair around to sit down. "I want to talk to you about your brother, Howard."

"Howard?"

"Yes, I saw you filed a missing person's report on him."

"That was years ago," Miriam said frowning. "Did you find him? He's not, the bones…"

"No, we don't know who that is yet. We just want to be ready if they ask for additional information."

"What kind of information?"

"Well, they are taking the recovered remains to the State Medical Examiner's office to see what they can learn from them. If they do confirm the bones are an adult male and find indications they might be about Howard's age, they will want samples to test for a possible identification."

"Oh, I see," Miriam murmured.

"Would you be willing to provide a DNA sample, if it comes to that?" Miriam's gaze was trained just below the edge of his desktop and the pause was far too long.

"No, Conrad," Miriam said raising her face up to meet his eyes. "I'm sorry, but no, I just can't do that."

"Well, Miriam, it doesn't have to be a blood draw or anything. It's just a simple swab of the inside of your cheek. It doesn't hurt."

"You'll have to find somebody else, Conrad. I'm not giving my DNA to the government."

"Why? What worries you, Miriam?"

"I don't trust the government to have it and I'm not going to voluntarily give it. That's all there is to it. Can I go now?"

"Wait, you said find somebody else. Are there other siblings in the area? Your parents?"

"My parents passed years ago," Miriam said standing and brushing imaginary lint from her skirt. "I do have a sister, but she doesn't live in Ohio."

"Can you give me her address or phone number?"

"Well, I don't know it off the top of my head," Miriam screeched and then lowered her voice. "I'll have to look. Maybe I have it around somewhere."

"I take it you aren't close with your family?"

Miriam scowled at his comment. "I'm sorry I can't help, but I've got to get going."

"What about his doctor or dentist? Do you know

if anyone has medical records on him?"

"Ask his wife," Miriam said as she stepped backwards toward the door. "She would know better than I would."

"I'm asking you," Conrad said impatiently.

"I don't know." Miriam fluffed her hair absentmindedly and looked out the office window. "We saw Dr. Hobbs as kids. Maybe he has old records. Howard had all kinds of health problems from his job in that filthy mine. I'm sure his prior employer knows who his medical provider was."

"What kind of health problems?"

"He was drawing disability checks from somewhere." Miriam threw up her hands in distaste. "Some kind of breathing problems, or that's what I heard. I don't know."

"You and Howard didn't talk much I gather."

"Don't judge me, Conrad," Miriam said pointing her finger. "I didn't approve of many things he did. We had little in common and no, I didn't pry into his private life. From what I know, it was rather sordid, but he was still my brother, so when I heard he had disappeared, I filed the report because his wife hadn't done it."

"I see," Conrad said demurely. "Well, thank you for stopping by."

Huffing at the dismissal, Miriam turned abruptly and stomped from the room. It was no wonder Cora Mae couldn't tolerate her.

Sheri Richey

CHAPTER 12

"Amanda?" Cora hollered from her desk to the outer office. "Do you have last year's parade list?"

"I'll get it." Cora heard filing cabinet drawers open up and shut several times before Amanda appeared with the list in hand.

"How many entries were there?"

"Uh, twenty-six," Amanda said handing Cora the list.

"Surely we can do better than that this year. What do you think about sending out some letters to businesses and community groups around the county? I'm thinking we might make it bigger this year if we invite some small towns around us to join in. They have school bands and clubs, too. I would like to see a really good crowd."

"Sounds like a great idea," Amanda said. "The carnival after and fireworks display will draw people from the neighboring towns, anyway. I'm sure they'd rather come here than go into Paxton. What about their Chamber of Commerce offices?

Maybe if we sent them some information, they'd share it with their members or give us a mailing list to use."

"Excellent idea," Cora said raising a fist in the air. She loved a parade and it would be especially exciting this year because of the statue dedication. The street department had decorated Main Street with potted spices and herbs. "Are my new spice labels going to get here on time? Jimmy has to have time get them all put around the downtown."

"They should be here next week," Amanda said. "We've already gotten an email that they've shipped."

"Oh, good. Put a note on my next agenda. I don't want to forget to give Jimmy Kole the details, so his employees know what we need. I told Jimmy about it but that was months ago."

"Will do."

"So, how are things at Bryan's now? Is everything getting back to normal?"

"Yes, the space people are gone," Amanda said chuckling. "They all wore white suits and masks out there. It looked like he was being invaded by aliens. He sure felt that way too."

"I'm glad that part is over for him. Was there much damage?"

"He thinks so," Amanda said rolling her eyes. "It doesn't look that bad to me. They basically chopped the corner off of that hill you go up and they took out two of his trees, which he was devastated about."

"Aw, that's a shame."

"Well, they didn't really hurt them because they weren't digging exactly. Anyway, he's trying to keep them alive and stabilize them so he can replant this weekend. I think it will be fine."

"Conrad said those new ones he planted were some kind of special tree, different from the others."

"Yes, they are Fraser Firs he has been babying for about four years. That's why he's all upset. The big trees in the back are all Scotch Pines. He's trying to branch out," Amanda said and then giggled at her pun. "He's hoping to offer a variety of tree types for Christmas in a few years.

Cora's eyes crinkled when she smiled. "Well, I hope they survive. I hope we all survive this craziness. At least they didn't find any other bodies up there."

"Yes, he had visions of them bulldozing his entire tree farm and he was about to have a heart attack over it. If it had turned out to be some ancient burial ground or something, his whole business would be gone."

"Being self-employed is a fragile state," Cora said handing the list back to Amanda. "I hope this doesn't cause him a big setback."

"Actually, it's made him kind of famous around town," Amanda said laughing. "Everybody knows about his business now."

"I guess any kind of publicity is good publicity."

"Oh, I forgot to tell you Rodney stopped by

early this morning before you came in. He's working on your picture, but he asked if he could add some things to the background. He thought it might look good to show him at a train station. Do we have any pictures of the old train station that was first here in Spicetown?"

"What a fabulous idea," Cora called out. "I love it! Yes, we have those pictures somewhere. We need to get them to Rodney."

"He did tell me one thing. He had one request."

"What was that?"

"He doesn't want his name on anything public," Amanda said shrugging. "He doesn't want any credit for anything because he doesn't want Carmen to know he's doing it."

"Hmm, he was serious about wanting to keep the money secret I guess," Cora said with a pinched brow. "I hate not giving him credit for his work though."

"I was a little surprised," Amanda said sitting down in the chair across from Cora's desk. "He actually was venting a little. He's not usually very talkative."

"Venting about what?"

"Oh, about all the commotion the bones have caused him. Apparently, everyone in town is talking about Carmen again. He said someone told her she was a suspect in the disappearance of Mavis' husband. Can you believe that?"

"Town gossip never surprises me," Cora said shaking her head. "Carmen can handle it. In fact, she's probably used to it, but it could really hurt her son."

"Oh yeah, he mentioned Andy. I think it already has gotten to him. He knows some people think his dad isn't his dad. I guess Rodney didn't even know her back then, but this has dredged up her past and he's having to hear about it from everybody."

"I'm sure she's not a suspect in anything," Cora said scoffing. "It's just that she's had a colorful past and a small town doesn't forget that."

"Well, he said he wants everyone to know Mavis' husband disappeared at Christmas time and Carmen wasn't even in town that year. She and her first husband were in Chicago visiting his family for the holidays."

"It's a shame he has to go through all this. Maybe we'll know something soon and this will all be over."

§

Conrad heard too much laughter coming down the hallway and decided he needed to investigate. Walking toward the dispatch room, he saw Georgia laughing and writing on a pad while several officers in the lounge laughed and shouted out unintelligible things.

"What's going on out here?" Conrad smiled but felt left out of the joke.

"You have some new phone messages," Georgia said smiling and holding out pink slips with one hand as she answered the phone with the other.

Conrad glanced at them and waited for Georgia to end her call. "You're very popular, Chief," Officer Tabor said with a chuckle.

"So," Georgia said spinning around to face Conrad. "Gilbert Tanner thinks it's his brother-in-law, Mark Decker. Norma Thomas thinks it's her neighbor's son, Nick Sloan. And Larry Conley thinks his wife may have killed her first husband, Donald Osburn." The lounge burst out in laughter and Georgia grinned. Conrad had been receiving similar messages for several days and it was escalating.

"I can't believe so many people have disappeared from Spicetown over the years."

"Oh, and the coroner called," Georgia said handing him another message. "She sounds like she has news."

"Good," Conrad said turning to walk back to his office. He was hoping for something that would define what was found so the calls would stop. "Don't you guys have anything to do?" Conrad called out as he walked away. Georgia giggled, but he heard the guys scuffle out the door.

Shifting through the folders spread across his desk as he dialed the phone, he looked for the names Georgia mentioned. Many of these calls hoping to identify the mysterious bones had named people who had never been reported missing in the police department records.

"This is Chief Harris. Can I speak to the coroner, please?"

"Conrad," Alice said in a hushed tone. "Just a second." Alice's voice was muffled as she told someone she needed to take his call.

"Sorry. I'm glad you called back. I've got some preliminary news and Sheriff Bell said you were helping do some leg work, so I told him I'd contact you."

"Thank you. I'm trying to help with what we have here at the PD. What do you know so far?"

"The bones are all washed, and we do have some small clues. It is an adult male, most likely Caucasian, about 5'11" tall."

"Hmm." Conrad looked over his desk and saw this really didn't disqualify hardly anyone yet.

"There is an old fracture though that might help us. It looks like he had a crush injury to his right ankle that may have required surgery. It's not too old. It's healed but looks like it happened in adulthood. Sometimes those surgeries use pins, plates, or screws, but we found no hardware. It could have been removed though."

"So, without the hardware—"

"Yes, we don't have a quick answer, but it was a significant injury so anyone knowing the person would have knowledge of it."

"That helps some," Conrad said. Once a time frame was found it could be really useful. "Would it impair his gait at all?"

"Not necessarily. It was healed and he could probably walk without difficulty. They are still sifting debris though so something else could turn up."

"I assume you don't have an age or an estimate on how long ago he died."

"No, but based on the soil, the forensic anthropologist agrees he's been there at least eight years.

"That's something," Conrad said as he pushed another file folder away from his possible pile.

"There are also some other indications of small fractures that may have been much older. His left ulna was broken probably as a child and some scarring on a few finger joints. The one thing still holding them up is the skull."

"I thought it was intact except for the jaw."

"Oh, it was, but it has damage. There is some debate about whether blunt force trauma is involved because of the location. There's some concern your young man, Bryan Stotlar, may have hit it with his shovel because the edges aren't clear. They're still working on that, so I'm not ready to call it a homicide yet."

"So, how can I help?"

"Well, we have the DNA extracted to start running matches if you have anyone lined up."

"You want me just to send a buccal swab kit to you when I get them?"

"Yes, that would be perfect. If we need more, we'll let you know."

"Will do," Conrad said cheerily. "And thank you again for letting me know."

With no cooperation from Miriam, Conrad took the only step he could and looked through his phone messages for Karen Goldman's phone number.

Sheri Richey

CHAPTER 13

"Hi, Amanda," Conrad said as he walked through Amanda's outer office and headed for Cora's open office door.

"Oh, Chief," Amanda said as he turned back. "She's not in there. She should be back any minute though."

"I can't find anybody today," Conrad said huffing.

"Can I help you?" Amanda smiled at this frustration.

"I was looking for Karen Goldman and she's not home. Miriam Landry isn't home or at the Chamber, but that woman—" Conrad huffed. "She's always hard to find. Then I went looking for Mavis and she's not at the drugstore. Now I'm here," Conrad said exasperatedly swinging his arms out to his side. "Of course, the Mayor's not here either."

"Oh, what are you in such a stew about now?" Cora said walking in Amanda's doorway with a chuckle. She'd watched his little performance and had to fight the urge to laugh. "I'm here now so you have finally met success."

Conrad laughed at his own performance when he saw Amanda trying to keep her face straight.

"Come in and sit down. No need to stress yourself out."

Conrad sat down hard in the chair across from Cora's desk and leaned forward with his elbows on his knees.

"So, I heard you've been chasing women all day," Cora said giggling. "What are you in such a flurry about? Don't you have people to do that?"

"Well, some things I just feel like I need to do myself."

"I assume you plan to talk about some sensitive information and none of those women are going to be easy to talk to right now."

"Karen Goldman has tried to be helpful. I just haven't been able to locate her today and she isn't answering her phone."

"She's probably at work. She's the manager down at the Sweet & Sour Spice Shop on Ginger Street."

"Well, I haven't been there yet," Conrad said shrugging and leaning back in the chair. "I don't think I want to talk to her at work though."

"I don't know where Miriam is," Cora said haughtily, "But if I did, I'd stay away from wherever that was." Conrad chuckled. Cora and Miriam had always butted heads over town events and after his recent conversation with Miriam, he understood why.

"I talked to her last week, but it took me several days to catch her. She was never at the Chamber when I checked in."

"She's probably just there for meetings. I don't know where she spends her days. Maybe she's off somewhere shopping," Cora said batting her eyes.

"Mavis may be off today," Conrad said as glanced over his shoulder at the open door. "I may have to go out to her house."

"Was Miriam cooperative when you talked to her last week?"

"No," Conrad said emphatically. "Not in the slightest bit. Does Howard Bell have any other family around here?"

"Maybe you should ask the Sheriff that," Cora said smiling.

"I'm not going there."

"I assume you are ready to talk about DNA?" Cora raised her eyebrows in question.

"Yeah, I need to see if there is anybody to test. I get a lot of people making suggestions, but nobody giving up any proof."

"You know, everyone says Andy Gentry is Howard's son.

"Yes, but unless a paternity test was done years ago to establish that, he's not a candidate either."

"Well," Cora said propping her elbows on her

desk. "They had a messy divorce. It's possible there was one."

"Does Andrew pay Carmen child support? Did he claim the boy? I thought officially he was Andrew's child. He has his name."

"Yes, he has his name and Carmen says he belongs to Andrew, but Andrew doesn't live around here anymore. I don't think he even kept in contact with the boy. Perhaps Carmen kept up the lie for appearances."

Conrad scowled. "I need to see if I can pull that court record."

"That's what I would do," Cora said smiling. "He's an adult now. He can make up his own mind about things."

Returning to his office, Conrad decided it was best to handle this the way he had with Miriam. He left a voice mail on Karen's phone that he'd like her to stop by his office. He left a message at the Chamber asking Miriam to call him with her sister's contact information and he started looking online at the county's website to see if he could obtain court documents. All this running around was exhausting him without anything to show for it.

Although he couldn't get the actual court documents, the court docket sheets were available to view, and he saw Carmen's divorce took over two years to complete. A paternity test was ordered on two different occasions but no results to the test were posted. There were several subpoenas issued for Carmen's medical records from various doctors without explanation. To make sense of all this, he would have to drive to Paxton and see the full file. Just having a paternity test ordered must mean the town gossip had reached Carmen's husband or his attorney because usually a child born during a marriage didn't have a question of paternity. This time it may be more than gossip.

§

"You're already here," Cora said in surprise when she saw Conrad waiting at their usual table. Conrad had called her office earlier to say he felt like a steak, so they had set a time to meet for dinner.

"Yes, I'm making a Cora Mae list."

Laughter trickled out as Cora pulled out a chair and sat down. "I do love a good list."

Conrad motioned to the waitress so she would see Cora had arrived. After giving the waitress her drink order, Cora wiggled out of her jacket and dug her glasses from her purse.

"What kind of list are we making?"

"I've got several people I need to see, and I have to keep all this straight. I want to make sure I ask all the questions I need to when I have them available. It seems I have trouble finding people lately," Conrad said scowling.

"Well, it is spring, and folks like to flit about when the weather is nice." Cora slipped her reading glasses on and took the paper Conrad offered.

"You may know some of these answers yourself, and if so, I'd appreciate your input."

"Hmm." Cora perused the list and tapped her finger on the name Dixie Martin. "My neighbor knew this girl. She came over to my house the day after it was in the paper and she was fretting about it."

"Her mother called me after the news came out about the bones," Conrad said glancing at the name Cora tapped. "I've got a copy of the report she filed."

"I'd say my neighbor may know more about her than her mother would."

"Well, that's less urgent since we know now that the victim was male."

"Maybe not," Cora said peering at Conrad over the top of her glasses. "She was allegedly in a relationship with Howard Bell when he disappeared."

"Oh," Conrad said leaning back in his chair. "Is this town gossip, too?"

"I hadn't heard it before. Sandy Nash lives across the street from me and she was Dixie's roommate back then. She's the one that told me."

"Speaking of Howard, he's the one I'm most concerned with. Do you know what you want?" Conrad said as the waitress approached.

"Welcome to the Barberry Tower." The young waitress gave them an anxious smile and lowered her head over her order pad. "Are you ready for me to take your order?"

Cora turned the list over on the table until the young woman had their order information, waiting until she walked away to resume.

"Do you know that young girl?" Conrad's eyes narrowed as he watched the waitress get drinks for another table. "She seemed pretty curious about what was on that paper."

"I can't remember her name. Alexa or Alyssa, something like that. She's Karen Goldman's step-daughter."

"Ah," Conrad said nodding.

"So why is Howard your main concern?"

"He's the only one Bobby has actually asked me to get involved in. He's worried about appearances because he has the same name. The others are just things I'm following up on because I've had citizens call in."

"So, the Sheriff is okay with you interviewing people in regard to Howard?"

"Yes," Conrad said lifting his water glass. "I'm doing my job, responding to general inquiries."

Cora gave him a quirky smile. Returning to the list, Cora pointed to another name. "Have you talked to Carmen?"

"Not yet. I've got a deputy running over to the courthouse tomorrow morning to pick up her divorce order from Andrew Gentry and I want to read that first."

"Well," Cora bellowed. "That will be a book. That drama lasted for years."

"I saw the docket and it was over two years long."

"Yes, with more drama even after it was final."

"So, where is Andrew Gentry? Does he live around here? I've never met him."

"I'm not sure," Cora said. "You know, I heard he was in West Virginia when the divorce was going on. He might be from there. He didn't grow up here in Spicetown. He moved here because of Carmen so when that fell apart, he left."

"He's not keeping in touch with the boy?"

"Not that I know of," Cora sneered. "Most people around here don't think it is his son. That's what ended the marriage."

"But the boy has his name."

"Yes, but I figured Carmen did that to save face. It was pretty common knowledge back then that their marriage was having trouble and Carmen began running around without Andrew. She liked to party, so her drunken exploits became beauty shop gossip. Later, the gossip started to involve Howard Bell, which surprised everybody."

"Why was that?"

"Well, Carmen was drawn to men with money. Andrew was well off and she had tried to fit in with the town's elite. She was pretty flashy. She liked to brag and show off what she had. Howard Bell didn't have anything," Cora said pausing to take a drink of her tea. "Except a family he couldn't afford to feed. He wasn't working and that's when Mavis took the job at Chervil's Drugstore to make some extra money. They were pretty stretched."

"Howard would have been a lot older."

"I think Carmen thought she'd get Andrew's money. She thought the baby would be her ticket, but she didn't get anything in that divorce. Andrew's money went toward a fancy lawyer, not to Carmen."

"So, if they were both married, how did everybody in town find out about it?"

"This is Spicetown," Cora said chuckling. "We have no secrets." When Cora saw their waitress returning, she turned the list over again and leaned toward Conrad. "At least none that escape the beauty shop."

Conrad laughed as the young woman distributed their dinners and bread basket before backing away.

"Tell me what you know about Howard," Conrad said as he put his napkin across his lap. "You said he didn't work?"

"He did when he married Mavis. For years he was a coal miner but then there was an accident in '98, I think," Cora said taking a quick bite of her chicken piccata.

"Was Howard injured?"

"Not that I know of, but after some people died in the accident, the mine closed. I think he'd worked there his whole life and that's all he knew."

117

"So, he was what? Forty-five back then? Too young to retire."

"I heard he had health problems, but I don't know any details. He may have had benefits from the mine, but I know the family needed money and that's why Mavis started working. She hadn't worked when the kids were young."

"But they aren't Howard's kids, right?" Conrad said slicing a piece of steak.

"No, Mavis was married before."

"Did he disappear, too?"

Cora laughed as she patted her mouth with her napkin. "Heavens, no. She was married to Clarence Ferrell when she had the kids. He died of cancer really young. Pancreatic cancer, if I remember right. The kids were little. They were only married about ten years before he got sick."

"So, Howard raised the kids?"

"I guess you could say so," Cora said sipping her tea. "I don't think it was very harmonious. Howard wasn't a good family man as it turned out. I rarely saw him. Mavis was the one that took care of the kids, came to all the school events and such. I had them both in class. Daniel was a bit surly, but Leanne was a bright girl. She's the oldest."

"Mavis told me at Bryan's grand opening that her daughter might move back here. She said she was hoping to have her grandkids close, but she didn't say where they were. She did say Daniel lived in Paxton now," Conrad said.

"Daniel is around all the time. I see him in town

so he may live over there, but he still has ties here. I think Leanne moved to St. Louis when she got married. She married Jack Summers and they moved when he got a job there. They were high school sweethearts and have a couple of kids, I think."

"Yes, two girls she said. Mavis didn't report Howard missing," Conrad said pushing his plate to the side and reaching for his coffee.

"No? Well, who did?"

Conrad chuckled and hesitated a moment. "Miriam Landry."

"Miriam?" Cora shrieked. "I can't believe she cared enough to even claim him. Everybody knows he is her brother, but she doesn't like to admit it."

"I didn't know it," Conrad shrugged. "She said she did it because Mavis didn't. She won't give a DNA sample though. I'm not sure why she filed the report because, like you say, she doesn't seem to care about him."

"Yes, that's peculiar. I would have never guessed she would involve herself in something so tedious."

The plates were gathered, and cups refilled as Cora pondered the list again. Conrad stretched back in his chair to push down his belt buckle and groaned.

"Are you planning to interview Carmen Maddox?" Cora said when the waitress left the table.

"Only if the divorce doesn't resolve the paternity

issue. If there was a test and the father wasn't Andrew, I may need to ask some tough questions."

"Well, if you do, I'd recommend you do it with Rodney present." Cora threw her hands up in front of her to deflect Conrad's objections. "I know you think I'm biased because I don't care for the woman, but I'm here to tell you she will lie to you for no reason at all. Rodney seems to be a rational person and you need a witness to what she says. If Bing were still here, he'd tell you the same."

"I take it you are speaking from his experiences?"

"I am," Cora nodded emphatically. "He had to interview her on more than one occasion, and she exhibits traits of a pathological liar. His words, not mine."

"Bing did give me some advice related to her," Conrad said looking down at his coffee. "He indicated she couldn't be trusted."

"He probably told you she'd flirt with you, but it's a bigger problem than that." Cora tipped her teacup up to get the last taste and then pushed the cup and saucer aside. "The problem is she will fabricate her interaction with you and you always need a witness. She made a lot of really inappropriate claims about Bing that he couldn't refute back in the day. I never believed them for a minute, but they tarnished his character in some eyes and he never put himself in that position again."

"I appreciate the warning."

"I can talk to Mavis for you, if you like," Cora offered. "She may be a little ticked with my prying right now, but she will talk to me candidly. I don't think I can help you with Miriam though."

Conrad laughed as the waitress brought them their checks.

CHAPTER 14

Before Conrad could get his coffeemaker dripping, Georgia was giving him more phone messages. The Sheriff's Department held a press conference the previous afternoon regarding the status of the Stotlar Nursery bones, which was the name the press had coined. This had stirred up the whole town again and now they were even calling him about missing friends and family members who had never been in Spicetown. Fortunately, Georgia handled these calls well and they rarely needed a call back.

"Chief, Karen Goldman is out here to see you." Officer Tabor looked at Conrad warily.

"Okay," Conrad nodded approval. "You can send her back here. Thanks."

Turning his coffeemaker on, he pulled out his desk chair and smiled as Karen entered the office.

"Thanks for coming in, Karen. Please have a seat."

Her eyes were darting all over the room, but she swiftly picked a chair. "I'm sorry it's so early, Chief. I'm shorthanded this week so I have to open the store."

"That's quite all right. I'm glad you were able to get in this quickly. I didn't want to bother you while you were at work."

"I guess this is about Uncle Howard? I saw the news last night."

"Yes, I have a few questions I need to ask you. We are trying to gather details about every possible missing person that could fit the description of what we have so far. They don't really have enough to make an identification yet. Any little detail might help."

"I want to help any way I can."

"Good. I hoped you'd say that," Conrad said smiling, as he opened his interview folder. "Let's get right to it because I know your time is limited." Conrad picked up a pen to make notes and sensed Karen was nervous, so he started off easily. "Can you tell me about your relationship with your uncle? Did you see him often?"

"I did when I was small. My Grandma Bell used to invite us to Sunday dinners, and we did all the holidays with her. Uncle Howard was always there then, and I remember when he married Mavis. Her daughter, Leanne, was my age and so we played together some."

"Is your grandmother still living?"

"Oh no," Karen said blowing out air through pursed lips. "She died when I was sixteen."

"So, is that when you stopped seeing Howard regularly?"

"It stopped a little before that," Karen said playing with the hem of her skirt. "We still did Christmas at Grandma's, but we didn't go visit much otherwise. When I was about thirteen, I guess, my mom and Howard had a falling out. They were arguing about something. I don't really know what, but I know we stopped going because of that. Then when Grandma died, that's when they stopped talking all together."

"But your mother is the one that filed the missing person report in 1999. Are you saying they weren't even speaking to each other at that point?"

"He was still her brother," Karen said in explanation. "I know she was upset Mavis hadn't reported it and she thought someone needed to."

"How did she know he was missing if she wasn't speaking to him?" Conrad tapped the end of his pen against the paper impatiently.

"Oh, the whole town knew. Everybody was talking about him disappearing because of Carmen Maddox. Well, she wasn't Maddox then. She was Carmen Gentry, but there was a lot of gossip about them having an affair. Leanne and I were seniors in high school back then and although we weren't really close, I know even the kids gave her a hard time about it. Mom was embarrassed."

"Did your mom try to talk to Mavis about it? See if she knew where he was?"

"I don't know," Karen said shrugging her shoulders. "Mom didn't really like Mavis, but she might have. I know she was really mad about all the gossip."

"Okay," Conrad said tapping the pad again and deciding to change direction. "Were you aware of your uncle having any specific health problems?"

"No, he seemed okay to me when I was a kid. You know, nobody really tells you anything when you're young. My mom would know," Karen said hesitating. "Maybe."

"What about children? I know he didn't have children with Mavis, but was he married before or do you know of any cousins…"

"Nope. As far as I know, Mavis was his only wife. I remember them getting married because it was the first wedding I had ever been to," Karen said smiling. "It was a big deal for me."

"To help us determine whether the remains could be your uncle, we will need some DNA to compare. Are you willing to take a DNA test? It's not a blood test or anything—"

"No," Karen said dropping her head to look at her clasped hands resting in her lap. "My mother, I know you already talked to my mother."

"Yes, and she wasn't willing to help us."

"I know," Karen said squeezing the fingers on one hand with the other. "She won't let me do it either."

"But Karen," Conrad said removing his reading glasses. "You are an adult and it's your decision."

"Yes, I mean no. It really isn't, Chief. She forbids it and I can't go against her. You see, I just can't do that. She insists and, well, it will just have to be someone else."

"Who should it be, Karen? Do you know how to contact your aunt? Your mother mentioned she has a sister."

"I don't. I've never really known Aunt Wanda. I mean, maybe I met her when I was young, but I don't remember. She and my mom don't get along."

"So, let me see if I understand this," Conrad said with a heavy sigh. "Your mom reported her brother missing, but now that there is a chance he may have been found, she is preventing anyone from confirming his identity. Do I have that right?"

Karen looked down at her hands again but remained still. "I can't explain it," Karen said looking up to meet Conrad's eyes. "My mother, well I just can't explain her, really. She's very commanding and if you go against her…"

"I tried to talk with your mother, Miriam, about this. She wasn't cooperative. I didn't realize she had such a long reach though," Conrad said. Karen looked helpless to stand against her mother.

"Something you should both understand though. This evidence can be subpoenaed if it becomes critical."

"Oh," Karen said with eyes bulging. "No, I didn't realize that. Well, then I could definitely do it then. It's not that I mind at all. I just don't want to lose my mom over it. She feels really strongly about it."

Conrad tossed his glasses onto his pad of paper and stretched back in his chair to hide his impatience. Miriam was a bully, plain and simple, and she had her only daughter intimidated. Conrad couldn't believe a mother would threaten to disconnect from her only child if that adult child didn't cooperate with her.

"Okay, thanks for stopping by," Conrad said, surprised Miriam permitted it. "I'll let the State Medical Examiner's office know we are unable to provide them a DNA sample because no one in your family will voluntarily submit. If they need something further, I'm sure they will take it to a judge so it can be ordered and served on Miriam." If being embarrassed in her community was what she feared most, Conrad hoped his words would get back to her so she would be prepared. He planned to make sure she was humiliated if he had the privilege to serve the subpoena. She deserved nothing less.

"I'll let her know," Karen said sweetly. "And again, Chief, I'm sorry I can't help more."

"It's not your fault, Karen," Conrad said

standing. "You have a good day."

§

"Mayor," Amanda called out as she walked to the open door of Cora's office. "Rodney is here. You said you had a picture of the train?"

"Oh, yes," Cora said excitedly. "Yes, Rodney, please come in. I'll get it for you." Bowing his head shyly, he entered the office.

"I was delighted when Amanda told me about your idea. I think it's a great plan and I'm excited to see it. I wish I had thought of it," Cora said beaming.

Pulling several photos from her desk drawer, she shuffled through them and selected one to hand to Rodney. "This is the first station." Rodney took the photo and peered closely.

"I also have a hand-drawn sketch of that same little building and another photo of a train. Now, the train photo dates a couple of years after John Spicer got here, but it will give you an example of how they looked in case you want to use them."

Still focusing closely on the photos, the silence was beginning to make Cora uncomfortable. "Please have a seat. Tell me what you think."

Rodney slid into one of the leather chairs across from Cora's desk but didn't seem to move his eyes off the photo.

"I'm sure you were imagining something much bigger," Cora smiled although Rodney didn't look up. "The original train station was just a tiny closet with a hook for the mailbag."

Amanda was standing in the doorway and Cora gave her a pleading look. The extended silence was excruciating.

"Would you like me to copy any of these, Rodney?" Amanda said shrugging at Cora.

"Yes, please," Rodney said snapping out of his trance. "I'd like to have all three. I haven't decided which would work best."

"Good idea," Cora said encouragingly. "So, how have you been, Rodney?"

"Fine," Rodney said nodding his head meekly.

"Amanda told me about keeping this hush-hush and I am happy to do that if that's what you truly want. I had planned to give you name credit on all the drawings."

"Oh, no ma'am. I don't need my name on anything. It's just tracing. I'm not an artist or anything."

"I beg to differ," Cora said emphatically. "I don't think you realize the majority of people cannot do what you can. It is very much a talent and you should be proud of it."

"Naw," Rodney said grinning uncomfortably from the compliment.

"Here you go." Amanda handed the copies to Rodney and the originals to Cora for filing.

"Is everything better at home now?" Cora asked

gingerly. "I mean with the bones being found and your wife being upset."

"Oh, well. I don't think it's much better yet. Maybe it will simmer down soon. My stepson is having some problems over it. People can be really mean sometimes."

"Yes," Cora said nodding sadly. "Yes, they can and I'm sorry you're going through this. Maybe when school gets out, he can get away from some of that."

Rodney just nodded his head meekly.

"Does Andy go visit his dad in the summers or does he stay here in town when school is out."

"He stays here," Rodney said rising from his chair. "Well, I better get going. Jimmy will want me on the job right away. Thank you for the photos. I'll get to work."

"Okay," Cora called as he walked out of her door. "Take care."

Frowning, she looked at Amanda. "Is it just me? Or does he not talk much?"

"He's pretty quiet," Amanda said. "But he even seemed more so today. He acts like he's got a lot on his mind. Maybe he's worried about this drawing."

"But adding all this difficulty to the drawing was his idea." Cora pulled out her drawer and slid the photos back into their file. "I just wish he wasn't so uncomfortable around me. I can't ever really seem to get him to talk. I know Carmen is having a hard time right now. The newspaper posted an article about the press release and then allowed people to comment online. There were some scathing things said that actually named her in some of them."

"Really? How rude."

"He was right about people being mean. It was totally unnecessary to mention that type of thing online. I felt sorry for her."

"I feel sorry for him anyway," Amanda said. "I don't think he has a very easy life."

"I guess not," Cora said wistfully.

CHAPTER 15

"Tabor is back, Chief," Georgia bellowed down the hallway as Conrad walked in the side door to the police station and turned to go to his office.

"Well, it's about time," Conrad mumbled. He had delayed going to lunch while he waited on him, but hunger finally overtook him.

"Sorry, Chief," Officer Eugene Tabor said when he appeared in Conrad's doorway. "I had to wait on them to copy it."

"It shouldn't take a half a day to do that," Conrad bellowed. "I thought you called them yesterday and asked them to get it ready."

"I did, but it's really big, Chief. And they kept showing me other stuff and asking me if I wanted it copied."

"What other stuff? I asked for a copy of the final order."

"I don't know what it all was. There were a bunch of orders for different things and I just kept telling them you needed the final order. Turns out there's like three of them though. Let me go get it."

Conrad was glad for the moment of peace so he could roll his eyes and take a calming breath before Eugene returned. Walking through the door, Officer Tabor held the copies in both hands and placed them in the center of Conrad's desk. The stack was almost two inches tall.

"This can't possibly be a court order," Conrad said strumming his fingers along the edges of the stack. "Or even three orders. They must have copied everything in the file."

"No, actually Chief, there were three different files. The original and then there were pleadings filed to reopen and revise the original order. That's why the clerk thought you would need all three. There are a bunch of exhibits attached to each one and she explained it all to me, but she seemed certain you would want it all."

"Okay," Conrad said pushing his chair away from the desk. "I guess this will take all afternoon. I better make coffee. Thank you, Tabor."

"Sure thing, Chief," Office Tabor said smiling as he disappeared from the doorway.

Pouring a cup from the pot he had made that morning, Conrad ran his hand over his thinning crew cut hair. He wasn't looking forward to this tedious job. He didn't need Carmen's life history. He had hoped to find this in an electronic searchable format so he could pick out what he wanted. This would definitely take all afternoon.

Glancing at the clock, he saw City Hall would be closing in less than three hours. He pulled a piece of paper from his notepad and added all the information listed for the petitioner, Andrew Gentry, to the list he had started earlier.

"Tabor," Conrad roared. He usually tried not to yell out his office door, but he could hear Officer Tabor chit-chatting with Georgia in the dispatch booth.

"Yeah, Chief?"

"Make me another copy of this," Conrad said plopping the thick volume back into Officer Tabor's hands. "And run these names for me." Conrad put the note on top of the stack. "I need to know where Andrew lives now. I need contact information for Wanda and a photocopy of this birth certificate."

"Right away, Chief."

Conrad ran his hands over his clean desk again, calmed the offensive volume was gone, and reached for the phone.

§

At the sound of the doorbell, Cora scooted to the front door in her house slippers and peered through the frosted glass. She had only been home long enough to kick her shoes off and feed

Marmalade, but she saw her dinner delivery had arrived.

"Hey, Connie. Just bring it in the kitchen. I haven't made any drinks yet."

Conrad slid the pizza box from Ole Thyme Italian Restaurant on her kitchen table. "I've got to run back out to the car to get the copies. I'll be right back."

Walking in with the two large stacks separated by a pad of paper, he slapped them down on the table.

"Goodness," Cora said placing her hand over her heart. "I can see why you weren't eager to dive right into all this."

"Yes, it looks ominous," Conrad said as he picked up the plates from the counter to place them on the table.

"Are these the transcripts?"

"Oh, no," Conrad said smiling. "These are just the final orders. There were three of them."

"The transcripts probably have their own dedicated storage room at the clerk's office. This divorce must have been bloody."

"A fitting analogy, but murder trials don't have this much paperwork."

"Well, here are the napkins," Cora said pulling out a kitchen chair. "Let's dive in."

"I talked to Miriam today," Conrad said between bites.

"Oh, how lovely for you." Cora snickered at her own sarcasm. "Did she bite your head off again?"

"She was surly. I may have permanently burned

a bridge with her. It was obvious her daughter had relayed my threat."

"She doesn't take kindly to anyone disagreeing with her or challenging her in any way. That's why we butt heads all the time. I tend to do both."

"I had left a message for her to call me, which of course she didn't do, so this afternoon I saw her parking to go in to the Chamber of Commerce office and I stopped her."

"Stopped her with your lights on?"

"Oh, no. I was walking down the street, so I just walked over. She immediately made a big fuss about being in a hurry and tried to run off, but I just followed her into the Chamber office."

"Shucks," Cora said chuckling. "I was hoping you pulled her over with your squad car right there on Paprika Parkway."

"It wasn't that dramatic, but the way she reacted, you would have thought I had."

"Was she any help?"

"No. She told me she'd look for her sister's contact information and get back to me. I had Eugene look up the sister, so I already have the info I need, but I wanted her to know it."

"So, she made all that fuss for nothing."

"Yep," Conrad said smiling. "I did drag it out a little though. I started off with reminding her of her promise to give me her sister's number and that I'd left a message with the Chamber secretary for her to call me. I wanted to let her flutter on about how busy she was and how she didn't know how to reach her sister. After she played out all of her excuses, I told her it was just fine because I'd already found her sister and had talked with her, so I didn't need anything further from her right now."

Cora's laughter burst out as she covered her mouth with a napkin. "Oh, how priceless. I wish I had seen it."

"I have to admit," Conrad said, dropping his chin, and wrinkling his nose. "I kind of enjoyed it."

"Is her sister, Wanda, anything like her?"

"No, not at all. She was actually a pleasant, cooperative, normal person. Nothing like Miriam."

"Her brother, Howard, always seemed nice, too. At least he was always friendly to me. Maybe he was a little too friendly to some of the ladies, but a regular guy. I don't know why Miriam is so evil."

"Once I told her sister that Miriam refused to cooperate in the identification process and that she had forbidden her only child to submit a DNA sample, Wanda couldn't wait to help me out. She's living down near Atlanta, so I called her local PD and they're going to take the sample for me."

"She's not a Miriam fan either?"

"She said she hadn't talked to her since their mother died. I got the impression she doesn't have any plans to speak to her ever again."

"Did she know Howard was missing? Did she ever talk to him?"

"I don't think so. She said she hadn't seen him in years either, but it didn't sound like she held any animosity toward him. They just weren't close, and she's always lived away."

"Well, at least you can mark one thing off your list. This should make Sheriff Bell happy."

"I'm going to wait until I actually have the kit in my hand before I count it a success, but I thought about shelving this whole Carmen development. The only reason I think I need to keep digging is if these bones really end up being Howard's, I want to have some background on the situation. If the bones aren't Howard's, I still have a missing persons case open in my office. Either way, I decided it needed to be done."

"I'm ready." Cora brushed the crumbs from her fingertips. "Would you rather move to the living room where it's more comfortable or stay at the table so you can take notes?"

"I'm fine here for right now."

Cora refilled their drinks and cleared the pizza plates from the table to prepare. "Your goal here is to answer the paternity question, correct?"

"Yes," Conrad said nodding his thanks for the drink. "Any proof of the adultery allegations might be useful too, in case the paternity issue isn't proven."

"Okay," Cora said, tossing a notebook of her own on the table and searching the kitchen drawer for a pen.

"To start off with," Conrad said as he pulled his reading glasses from his shirt pocket. "You'll notice Andrew filed the action and he's making an adultery allegation. This isn't a no-fault divorce or a mutual request for dissolution. Carmen obviously didn't want the divorce. That's probably why it dragged on so long."

Cora hummed softly and began scanning the first few pages to catch up. The sound of pens scratching across paper was interrupted only by an occasional complaint from Marmalade that she needed attention. When Conrad finished reading, he stood up and stretched his back out with a groan.

"Would you like me to make you some coffee?" Cora said.

"No thank you. It'll just keep me up tonight. Although reading this will probably give me nightmares."

"It is very scathing," Cora said sadly. "It had to be a very painful two years for them both." Cora stood and went to the counter to rinse out her teacup. "Let's go in the living room. I'd like to put my feet up."

Conrad chose the recliner which had been Bing's favorite. Since her husband's death, she had privately had more than a few conversations with that chair, wishing he was still there to advise her. Cora preferred the wingback with a matching ottoman that sat beside an end table separating her from the recliner. Turning on the lamp between them, she kicked off her house shoes and put her feet up on the footstool.

"Gloominess aside," Conrad said flipping through his notes. "We did learn a few things."

"Yes, along with a lot of stuff we didn't want to know." Cora raised her eyebrows sheepishly.

Conrad cleared his throat to avoid a grin and tilted his head back for a better focus through his reading glasses. "Adultery was the primary allegation, but it wasn't just Howard Bell."

"I noticed that, but I have to say I was most shocked to see Rodney Maddox named in there. I didn't even know he knew Carmen back then. I just asked him the other day how long he'd been married, and he told me it's been ten years."

"When I moved here, I thought Carmen was dating Paul Henson. I didn't meet Rodney until after he married Carmen and came to work for the city."

"As far as I know, Rodney was married before. Maybe they dated and he thought she was separated."

"Then he ends up in a court document," Conrad said flipping another page over.

"Andrew asked for a paternity test twice and the judge ordered it, but it was never performed. I wondered why the judge subpoenaed medical records for Carmen. I saw that in the docket sheet online. You don't usually see that in a divorce."

"Carmen must have had a great attorney to get out of that because it would have been easy to test the baby at the hospital when he was born. I noticed the first order was during the pregnancy and the second was after."

"It sounds like Andrew shot himself in his own

foot on that one," Conrad said shifting in his chair. "If he buys the baby stuff and visits the baby, the judge is going to be inclined to make the baby his. I had Andy's birth certificate pulled and Andrew is on it."

"So, your original goal was to see if paternity was determined. Little Andy can't help you with DNA," Cora said, but then shifted in her chair to point a finger at Conrad. "You know, Andy is an adult now and Rodney told me his father isn't in the picture, so he won't have any allegiance to him. He might want to consent to a test just for his own curiosity. I wonder how he gets along with his mother."

"Reading between the lines here, it looks to me like Andrew paid her off."

"What do you mean?"

"He paid her attorney fees, he offered her alimony, and then he gave her the house. He just wanted out and didn't want to be tied down with a baby—"

"That he didn't think was his," Cora said finishing Conrad's sentence. "It was abrupt, too. I mean, didn't you think they haggled for months and months before everything fell into place at once? Maybe it's just how it reads, but that seems odd. Like we don't know something. We're missing some piece to this puzzle."

"Please don't tell me I need to read the whole file," Conrad said with an exaggerated grimace.

"No, it's faster to pull it out of someone.

Someone knows. Carmen won't help, but Rodney, Andy or even Andrew might. I have a feeling the truth isn't even in the file."

CHAPTER 16

Conrad pulled his car into Cora's driveway on Saturday morning and even though he saw her coming out of the side door, he honked the horn. It made her flap her hands in the air to scold him and he found it amusing. Still chuckling when she slid in the passenger seat, he waited for her to arrange her purse in the floor and get her seatbelt on before he put the car in reverse.

"Did you tell Amanda you were going by the nursery today?"

"No, I didn't get a chance, but she'll probably be there. I think she's out there working every minute she's not at City Hall."

"Does he have any employees hired yet?"

"As a matter of fact, he does," Cora said with a satisfied smile. "Leanne Summers is working there during the day and Mavis is there part-time when she's not scheduled at the drugstore."

"Leanne is Mavis' daughter?"

"Yes. She's working during the day when her kids are in school. She's just moved them here. That may change when school lets out though."

"That should make Mavis happy. She was hoping to talk her daughter into moving home."

"Yes, but I didn't know she meant she wanted Leanne to move in her house. I thought she wanted them to move closer so she could see the kids. Leanne has moved in and her husband didn't come."

"Are they splitting up or is he coming later?"

"I don't know for sure. All I heard was petty gossip and speculation."

"Is this beauty shop talk again?" Conrad shook his head and scowled. Cora did pick up some of the best information at Louise's Beauty Shop. Amanda's mother, Louise, ran a popular hair salon a block off Fennel Street and all the world's problems were solved there.

"Yes, but Amanda confirmed she is working there."

"I may not need to go to Mavis' house then. She may be here," Conrad said as they pulled across the gravel parking lot.

"I'll introduce you to Leanne."

Parking toward the back of the lot and walking up to the nursery, Conrad could not help noticing the cars they passed. His eyes were always trained on license plates from years of habit, but he could identify many of the town residents just by their vehicles. Seeing a license plate from West Virginia gave him pause.

"I can see Amanda from here," Cora said as they approached.

"Oh, hi Mayor. Chief," Rodney said with a one-finger salute as he walked past.

"Are you leaving?" Cora called out. He seemed to be in a hurry and didn't even pause when he greeted them.

"No, ma'am. Just getting some tools from my truck."

"He must be doing some work here today," Cora said in a half whisper.

"Mayor," Amanda said waving her hand over her head. She was behind a table covered in small yard bushes and flowering plants. Stopping to look around, Conrad saw Mavis bent over some plants sitting on the pavement. She had a large plastic water can tipped over and was holding it with both hands.

"You've been busy today?" Cora asked Amanda as they approached.

"We have," Amanda said smiling. "Saturday's are always the best."

Conrad had been trailing Cora but wandered off when he saw Bryan on the side of the greenhouse.

143

"How has everything been going?"

"Pretty good," Bryan said taking a deep breath. "It's hard work, though."

"Starting any business will be, but yours will probably always involve a lot of labor. Has everything returned to normal?"

"My garden will never be the same," Bryan said snidely. "Come see it. They took at least a half a ton of dirt out of the side."

Following Bryan around the greenhouse, Conrad could see from a distance that the slope he had walked up earlier was no longer there.

"They dug out the whole side of the plot. I had to move three of my small trees and one was destroyed. It's a mess out here. I guess they had to make sure there was no one else in there."

"They have to sift through the surrounding soil to look for trace evidence." Conrad had recently received a report from Alice with a list of items found with the remains. There were small metal items, buttons from clothing and shoes, but no medical hardware that would help with identification.

"I have a guy coming tomorrow to bring me some fill dirt for the surrounding area and I ordered some soil to help patch the garden. I'm trying to get it back to normal."

Conrad looked over his shoulder and saw Cora standing by the bell.

"Hey, Mayor. How are you?" Bryan said when he noticed her standing there. "Ring the bell for service. Can I help you with something?"

Cora pointed to the sign under the bell. "Did you see this Chief? Did Rodney make this sign for you? We passed him on our way in." A small wooden plaque had been nailed to the post that held the bell. It had been carved and painted, much like the business sign at the road, saying "Ring Bell for Service".

"Yeah, he made it. Pretty neat idea and it looks nice. My mom used to ring that bell when she wanted my dad and couldn't find him. It was already here on the farm when they bought it. Of course, I was always messing with it when I was a kid," Bryan said apologetically. "I probably drove the neighbors crazy."

"I decided I needed another screw on the bottom," Rodney said as he walked up with a small toolbox in his hand.

"I love your sign, Rodney," Cora said stepping aside so he could finish attaching it to the post. "We were just talking about it."

"Thank you."

"I thought it would come in handy if people show up during the day when I'm working alone and I'm back here in the trees or the garden somewhere." Bryan pointed to the front lot. "I told Amanda we might ought to get one for the front, too."

"You'll have all the kids playing on it just like you did, though," Conrad said with a chuckle.

"If you've got a minute, Chief," Bryan said as he

walked down the incline. "I've got something in the house I'd like to show you."

"Sure," Conrad said patting him on the shoulder and following Bryan as he walked towards the house.

"I wanted to show you the paperwork the State gave me when they left. It's a lot of legal jargon and I can't make anything of it. My question is, do I have to pay to repair the damage they caused?"

"Hmm, I don't really know, Bryan," Conrad said chuckling. "It's never come up before. Let me take a look, but you may need to see an attorney. It's possible your homeowner's insurance might cover it, too."

"I hadn't thought of that."

"Bryan," Mavis called out through the screen door. "Oh, hi there, Chief. I didn't know you were here."

"Come on in, Mavis." Bryan walked to the door to open it.

"That's okay," Mavis said stepping back when Bryan pushed open the door. "I don't want to interrupt. I was just going to ask if you were done with the hose you have out back. I need to move it around and do the front tables."

"Oh, sure. That's fine. You can take it. Hey, Mavis, isn't your son-in-law a lawyer?"

"No," Mavis said hesitatingly. "He works for an attorney in St. Louis, but he doesn't have a law degree."

"Oh, I was thinking he did," Bryan said. "Never

mind, then. I was just looking for legal advice."

"Okay. Let me get back to work," Mavis said quickly bowing out the door.

"Cora told me Leanne was living next door now," Conrad said once Mavis was several paces away. "Is her husband moving here, too?"

"I'm not sure. They both give me mixed answers on that. I thought maybe they were having some problems."

"Do you know Jack?" Conrad asked. "I've never met him."

"Yeah, I haven't seen him in years, since I was in high school, but I knew him then. He was always over at the house next door."

"I do need to talk to Mavis sometime today. I have some questions about her husband, and I haven't been able to catch her this week. What time does she get off?"

"Oh, if you need to talk to her, go right ahead. Leanne is helping Amanda out and we'll be fine. You don't have to wait."

"Thank you," Conrad said. "And if you don't have an attorney to talk to, have Amanda make me a copy of this and I'll ask Ned Carey to give it a glance. He's a coffee buddy of mine and he can decipher it for you. He's done lots of contract work and maybe it will make some sense to him."

"Great," Bryan said holding the door open for Conrad. "Thanks, Chief."

"Oh, I think someone is ringing your bell," Conrad said smiling as he heard the chimes begin when they walked outside. Bryan might be sorry he put that sign up there after all.

§

When Bryan and Conrad walked in the house, Cora remained standing next to the bell watching Rodney work to add a screw holding the bottom of the sign. "So, are you working out here part-time now?"

"Yeah," Rodney said grunting as he turned the screwdriver. "Just until Bryan is all set up. I'm hoping he gets some landscaping jobs and I'll be able to help out there."

"Working on getting that tree, huh?"

"Yep," Rodney smiled. "Have you seen it? It's out front. It doesn't look like much right now, but in the fall, it's a beauty."

"Does Andy like working out in the yard with you?"

"Naw, not much," Rodney said as he dropped the screw driver and took his hammer out of his toolbox. "I mean he can help mow, but he doesn't really like it."

"Oh, I thought maybe this would be a good summer job for him out here or on landscaping jobs. You could work together."

"Yeah, I wish he liked that kind of stuff. He'd rather sit around and play video games or drive around town in a circle." Rodney laughed and shook his head.

"So, what are his plans? He's going to graduate this year, right?"

"Yeah, in just a few months," Rodney said as he looked down at his toolbox again. "You'll have to excuse me, Mayor. I've got to run out to my truck again."

"Of course, go ahead," Cora said politely. She planned to wait right there until he returned. He was dodging a simple question anyone would ask of a parent with a child graduating high school and she wasn't going to let him get away with it.

"Mavis," Cora cried out when she saw Mavis Bell coming around the corner of the greenhouse. "How are you?"

"I'm good, Cora Mae. What are you up to today?"

"Oh, just running around. I thought I'd come out and check on the kids today. Looks like things are getting back to normal."

Mavis pulled the long water hose away from the house and then paused. "I wanted to apologize to you," Mavis said.

"Well, whatever for?"

"The last time we spoke, when you came in the store, I was pretty short with you and I apologize. I know you don't mean no harm."

"Certainly not, Mavis. I would never mean to cause you any harm. My questions may have seemed insensitive and for that, I owe you an apology."

"No, no. It was just a bad day, you see. People kept coming in because they heard the news and they wanted to open up all that old can of worms. I shouldn't have let it get to me."

"I know it's had to be hard on you. I wish I could say it's over, but I know the Chief needs to talk to you. I hope you'll help him gather the information he needs."

"For sure," Mavis said. "I don't mean to be a problem. What does the Chief need?"

"I think he needs to try to find dental or medical records for Howard. He has questions about the timeframe and what was going on back then. You know, he didn't live here then. He didn't ever know Howard."

"Oh, I'm happy to help him. You know, Cora Mae, I never believed anything bad happened to Howard. Still don't. I think he just left town. He just left me. Miriam tried to make a big deal out of it, but it wasn't nothing but a squabble between husband and wife. It was nothing for her to concern herself with. She never paid us any mind before that. Then all of a sudden, she's sticking her nose into everything and making people think the worst. She was the one spreading gossip everywhere and she always said she hated gossip."

"I know Miriam can be trying to deal with," Cora said. "She has a very strong personality."

"It's all happening again. Everybody thinks those bones up there were Howard's—"

"But you don't?"

"No," Mavis said shaking her head sharply. "Nobody wanted to kill Howard. He wasn't causing anybody any harm, except maybe me." Mavis chuckled and ran her hand through her hair. "And it wasn't me."

"That's good to know," Cora said smiling.

"Even I didn't want to kill him. I loved him. He wasn't perfect. None of us are, but he did run around on me some and that was hard to take, but I never kicked him out."

Cora shook her head quizzically.

"No, I didn't want him to leave. He was just restless, down on his luck, you know? After the mine closed and he couldn't find work, he didn't feel, well, you know how men are about thinking they need to be the bread winner. They need to take care of their family and he couldn't. He had a hard time of it when I went to work at the drugstore. It made him feel like less of a man."

"How did the kids handle it? They were pretty young. First, they lose a father and then Howard is gone."

"Well, they were old enough to understand," Mavis said as she wiped her hands off on the tail of her shirt. "They never did get close to Howard. Maybe they were afraid to do that after they lost their dad. I don't know, but teenagers, even under normal circumstances, are hard to handle."

"It looks like you've done a fine job," Cora said smiling at Leanne as she approached. "How are you doing, Leanne? It's good to see you."

"Are you talking about me?" Leanne teased her mother. "I can always tell by that look on your face." Mavis laughed as Leanne put an arm around her.

"Do you remember Cora Mae?" Mavis asked Leanne. "She was your teacher—"

"Mrs. Bingham," Leanne said smiling. "Yes, I remember."

"It's Mayor Bingham now," Mavis said proudly.

"Wow. No, I didn't know. I've been away a long time."

"You can call me Cora Mae, just like your mother does. That's still my name. I'm glad to see you've come home. I know your mom loves having you here."

"I never thought I would live here again, but since I've been back, I'm enjoying it. I get to see my brother, Daniel, and so far, it's been pretty fun working here. My girls really like the school and I think it's a good place for us."

"That's great," Cora said. "Spicetown is happy to have you. Is Jack coming, too?"

"I don't think so," Leanne said squeezing her mother's shoulders before releasing her. "He plans to stay in St. Louis. Maybe he'll change his mind, but right now we just need some time apart."

"I understand," Cora said sincerely. "Sometimes it's the best thing to help you work things out."

"Well, let me get this hose moved," Mavis said pulling on it and Leanne jumped to help. "It was good to see you, Cora. You tell the Chief I'm happy to help."

"I will, Mavis. You two take care now."

As the two ladies wrestled the long water hose, Conrad walked around the side of the greenhouse and stopped to help by taking the hose from them and pulling it to the front of the building while Cora waited for Rodney to return.

CHAPTER 17

"Here, Mom," Leanne said taking the hose from Mavis' hand. "Let me. I'll water the bushes on the side. Thank you for the help, Chief. I've got it." Leanne pulled the hose up in a loop and walked on trusting the rest would follow.

"Mavis, if you've got a few minutes, I do have some questions I need to ask you. Bryan said it was okay if you take a little break."

"Sure, Chief. Cora said you needed to talk to me. I'm happy to help. Do you want to go inside?"

"Yes, that might be best," Conrad said as they walked around the front of the greenhouse and back behind the potting tables to find a small seating area. "As you may already know, the State is trying to ID the man Bryan found buried in his garden."

Mavis nodded and closed her eyes briefly.

"To help them out," Conrad pulled a pen and a

small notebook from his pocket, "they've asked for some DNA samples to test against the remains."

"I'm afraid I don't have much to offer you, Chief. It's been a really long time and when Howard didn't come back, I have pretty much gotten rid of this clothing."

"Oh, that's okay, Mavis. What I'm needing is more in line with some direction as to where I can find information on Howard."

"What kind of information?" Mavis asked wrinkling her nose.

"Tell me about his health. Was he seeing any doctors? Did he have any problems?"

"Well, he was over fifty, so you know what that means," Mavis said smiling. "Things start to go on you."

"What kind of problems did Howard have?"

"He had some arthritis and asthma. His back was stiff and sore a lot, but he had worked hard all his life. His cholesterol was too high, and he took a blood pressure pill."

"Who was his treating physician?"

"He saw a guy over in Red River," Mavis said shaking her head. "I can't remember his name, but I might have it at home. He had to go over there to have his insurance cover it. That guy saw all the miners, but I can't remember his name. It's something weird, like, uh, Pajamas, Palola, Pagala. Something like that."

"Did he take any other medication?"

"He had an inhaler, but he only used it when he

needed to."

"Were his medications still at home after he disappeared?"

"Yeah, except for the inhaler. The pills were there."

"What about broken bones, surgeries, dental work? Anything like that?"

"He had Dr. Hobbs pull a tooth for him once, but that was when he was still working. No surgeries though." Mavis reached over to stroke the broad leaf of a plant sitting on the table. "At least not while we were married."

"So, he wasn't disabled," Conrad said trying to catch Mavis' eye as she looked around the room. "He was healthy enough to work, right?"

"Oh, sure," Mavis said turning back to nod at Conrad. "It's just when his mine closed, there wasn't anything else around hiring. That's all he'd ever done."

"What about hobbies? What did he spend his time on during the day after he wasn't working?"

Mavis stared at Conrad in a stunned silence.

"Did he like to tinker on cars or build things? You know, did he have household repairs to do? What did he do during the day?"

"He really didn't have any hobbies," Mavis said shrugging. "He'd always worked long hours but when the mine closed, I went to work at Chervil's, so I was gone all day. As far as I know he just watched TV."

"When did the mine close?" Conrad asked

frowning. It was a distant memory, but he couldn't recall the circumstances.

"In September of '99," Mavis said shaking her head woefully. "There was an accident. An awful accident and two guys were killed when the roof collapsed. Howard was there when it happened, but he wasn't injured. Several were, but the State had just been there and inspected. They said it was safe. They don't know why it happened."

"I didn't realize," Conrad said somberly. "I wasn't living here then, and I just recall there was a shutdown."

"Yes, the closing was announced back in the spring of '99 and they laid off most of the workers then, so Howard knew it was coming, but he was fortunate they kept him on to help with closing. He'd been with them for a long time."

"Okay," Conrad said shifting in his chair and deciding to shift the conversation as well. "When was the last time you saw him?"

Mavis lifted her face and glared at a spot above Conrad's head. "I left for work at 9:00 on the morning of December 17th in 1999. He was sitting in his favorite arm chair with the TV Guide. We had just had breakfast. I think it was a Friday." Conrad made some notes and remained quiet, feeling the trance Mavis was in had more to reveal than any questions he might ask. "The kids had already left for school. I remember it was warm that day. Unusually warm for a December day and I just had on a light jacket. We talked about

Christmas, about how it was too warm to be Christmas time and what I would make for dinner. He asked when I'd be home." Mavis looked down at her hands in her lap. "Just the usual stuff. Nothing special. I thought he'd be sitting right there when I got home."

"You've thought about it a lot," Conrad said nodding. Her response had a pre-recorded feel to it, but he didn't think it was for his benefit. He thought it was a scene she'd played over in her mind many times.

"I have. It was a completely normal day. Nothing special at all."

"Did the kids get home before you did that day?"

"I think so. They didn't always, but it seems like they were there and asked where Howard was. They said he wasn't home when they got there."

"Were you concerned then?"

"No, not really. I mean he did go to town once in a while, run an errand or have a drink, and I didn't really know. I mean I never expected him to not come home or anything. His clothes were all still there."

"So, there wasn't a problem? You weren't in any disagreement with him or anything?"

"Not that day," Mavis said and chuckled. "We had our fights from time to time, but I don't remember one that day."

"Did your children get along well with Howard? He practically raised them, didn't he?"

"They were teenagers. Nobody got along well

with them," Mavis said smirking. "Their dad died when they were young, but they remember Clarence. They couldn't remember much, but they never accepted Howard as their dad or anything. They always referred to him as their stepfather."

"Were there any ongoing disagreements between Howard and the children?"

"Yeah, of course there were. Howard was strict. He didn't like Leanne running around town with Jack when no one knew where she was. He didn't like Daniel's attitude sometimes. Stuff like that. Typical teenager problems."

"All of this was before my time," Conrad said with a sympathetic shrug. "I never got to meet Howard. I just met Leanne for the first time today. Is Jack her husband?"

"Yeah, he is now. They dated in high school."

"So, I guess you saw a lot of him back then, too? Did he and Howard get along okay?"

"Jack wasn't at the house much. All parents worry about their young girls dating. Nothing more than the normal."

"Howard never had any children of his own?"

"No. He'd never been married before."

"Was Howard involved with anyone?" Conrad had hoped Mavis would volunteer this information, but he couldn't let it stand unaddressed.

"Rumors," Mavis said with a wave of her hand. "People in town told me he'd been seen with other women, but no. I don't know that to be true."

"Did you ask him about it?"

"Sure," Mavis said heartily. "In the beginning, I asked him every time I heard a rumor about it. He always denied it and I never saw any evidence of it either. Eventually, I just quit asking."

"So, you didn't think he was in a relationship with anybody in particular when he disappeared," Conrad said as a statement to confirm her answer, rather than a question.

"No," Mavis said shaking her head. "People talked about him being with some young girl and I didn't believe that. He wouldn't cavort around with someone half his age. He wasn't having an affair with Carmen Gentry either." Mavis scoffed. "She flirted with everyone. Her name was linked to every married man in town."

"If Howard was really having an affair, would that have ended your marriage?"

"I don't know," Mavis said wistfully. "He did cheat on me once and I knew he did, but I forgave him. He said he wouldn't do it again and as far as I know he didn't. I guess it would just depend."

"When was that?"

"Oh, back when we were just married. Well, maybe after we'd been married a couple of years. I don't remember exactly but the kids were still young."

"Do you think those bones belong to Howard?" Conrad saw he had shocked Mavis with that question, but she paused long enough to consider it.

"I don't."

"Where do you think Howard is?"

"I don't rightly know, Chief," Mavis said with a pointed glare. "But I don't think he's dead. I've lived all these years waiting and it wouldn't surprise me a bit if he just walked through my door one day."

"Well, I hope you're right, Mavis," Conrad said smiling. "That's all the questions I have right now. I'll let you know if I need anything else."

"Sure thing, Chief. I better get back to work." Mavis popped up out of her chair and swiftly left the greenhouse leaving Conrad staring at his notepad.

§

"Amanda," Cora said walking up to peer over Amanda's shoulder as she scooped potting soil into a ceramic flower pot. "Have you seen Rodney? He was working on the sign by the bell and said he had to get something from his truck, but I've never seen him come back."

"No, I haven't seen him for a while. Did you need him?"

"Not really," Cora said chewing her bottom lip. "I think he's avoiding me."

Amanda laughed and glanced back at Cora.

"What are you ladies up to?" Conrad said as he

strolled up with a tray of tiny plants in his hands.

"Have you decided to take up gardening, Chief?" Amanda brushed the dirt of her hands and picked up a towel to wipe the sides of the ceramic pot clean.

"Not yet," Conrad said smiling. "I told Georgia Marks I'd pick these up for her when I was out here. She likes to grow her own tomatoes and she's working today."

"They do taste better from your own garden," Cora said as she saw Daniel Farrell approaching. "Hi, Daniel. How are you?"

"Good. Good. Amanda, do you know where my sister is?"

Amanda glanced around the front displays but didn't see Leanne anywhere.

"Chief, this is Daniel Farrell, Mavis' son."

Conrad extended his hand to shake and after a hesitant glance, Daniel reciprocated. "Conrad Harris. It's nice to meet you, Daniel."

"You too, Chief. Sorry, I've got to run. I need to find Leanne."

"Check in the greenhouse," Amanda suggested as Daniel nodded and took off in a trot. "I wonder what that's about."

"Hmm, I'd say it's about Jack Summers," Cora said angling her head and motioning with her eyes as Leanne's husband walked up the middle of the parking lot.

"Is that Leanne's husband?" Amanda said discreetly.

"Yes," Cora said smiling. "And he's supposed to be in St. Louis."

"Oh my," Amanda said with a worrying frown. "Is that going to be a problem?"

"I don't know, but having the Chief here can't hurt," Cora said glancing at Conrad and chuckling.

"I was about to ask if you were ready to go," Conrad said hesitantly. "But maybe we ought to wait a bit."

"So, what are you planting, uh, or potting, here," Cora said waving her hands over Amanda's project.

"It's a houseplant called a Flamingo Flower," Amanda said smiling. "They bloom inside several weeks out of the year and have these pretty heart-shaped leaves."

"I've never heard of it," Cora said frowning as Amanda put a small plastic spike in the soil with a skull and bones on it. "What's that?"

"Just a warning flag," Amanda said pulling the spike out to show Cora. "It's toxic to animals so we want people to know it's not a good choice to buy if you have pets."

"Maybe the skull and bones are not the best way to convey that message," Cora said winking at Amanda. "I mean, considering the grand opening discovery."

Amanda tossed her head back in laughter and Cora was glad to see the previous tensions from the event had subsided. "Maybe not," Amanda agreed. "I'll mention it to Bryan."

"There goes Daniel," Conrad muttered as they

watched Daniel stomp briskly across the parking lot with his head down. "He seems rather agitated."

"Hmm," Cora hummed as she craned her neck to peer around the plants. "I don't see Leanne and Jack anywhere."

"If you'll watch Georgia's tomatoes, I'll go check the greenhouse," Conrad said and turned to Amanda. "If someone asks, what might I be looking for in there?"

Amanda laughed again. "Well, Chief, I'd recommend a tomato cage. We have them in there and it would go well with your purchase."

"Ah, good idea," Conrad said walking off without any idea what a tomato cage looked like.

CHAPTER 18

As Conrad approached the greenhouse, he saw Leanne and Jack behind the building standing near the garden bell. Their postures easily conveyed tension, but Conrad didn't see any threat of violence, so he turned in the door to the greenhouse and looked around. He could hear Jack's voice because he was facing the greenhouse but much of it was muffled. Standing just inside the door, he pretended to be seriously considering a potted plant as his ears remained trained to the action happening by the bell in the garden.

"Can I help you with something, Chief?" Bryan appeared at Conrad's elbow and looked down at the plant Conrad was focused on. "That's a peace lily, Chief. A good choice for a peace officer," Bryan said smiling. "They make a nice office plant."

Conrad stared blankly at Bryan and then glanced

down at the plant. "Oh, no. Actually, I'm just, well... uh."

"They make a wonderful gift too," Bryan said. "They bloom year around."

"Well," Conrad said leaning toward Bryan and lowering his voice. "I'm actually just keeping an ear out for the couple at the bell. The ladies were a little concerned there might be some trouble there, so I just wanted to hang close by."

Bryan stepped to the greenhouse doorway and surveyed the area before stepping back inside and nodding. "Jack Summers is here."

"Yes," Conrad said waiting for a reaction from Bryan.

"I don't think there's anything to worry about," Bryan said lifting a shoulder in a half shrug. "Jack's pretty easy-going. Leanne's the mean one of that pair. Jack usually does exactly what he's told to do. If she's mad at him, I'm sure he must have disobeyed."

"I don't know either of them," Conrad shook his head and took a deep breath. "Maybe the ladies were just concerned because his arrival was a surprise."

"I know they're having some trouble," Bryan said as he rearranged some small planters. "She's thinking about moving back here. I don't think anything's definite yet though."

"You knew Daniel and Leanne growing up, I guess."

"Yeah, they were both older, so we weren't

friends or anything, but I saw them around all the time. Daniel still visits Mavis pretty regularly, but I hadn't seen Leanne in almost a year."

"So, her job here is just temporary?"

"Yes. She just came over with her mom one day. We talked about it and she's going to work a few hours during the week while her kids are at school so I can get some planting done."

"That means I guess you knew Howard Bell, too?"

"Oh, yeah. I mean I was a kid, so I didn't talk to him or anything, but he came over and talked to Dad some. Usually he was looking for Daniel, but they talked about the animals and helped each other sometimes, too."

"Was Daniel over here often?"

"No, he had a four-wheeler and dad let him ride on our land in the back, so Howard would walk over here looking for him when he needed him to come home. He'd ring the bell and if that didn't work, he'd walk back behind the gardens to see if he could find him. The Christmas trees weren't there back then."

"Did Leanne and Daniel get along well with Howard? I mean, do you know? Did they like him?"

"They didn't seem to," Bryan said huffing. "They were always bickering. Howard always seemed mad at them and they would talk back to him. In Howard's defense, both of those kids were a real handful. I was always a little afraid of getting in their way."

Conrad heard Leanne's voice getting louder and picked up the plant to hold it out to Bryan. He wanted to look engaged in something when they walked by.

"I'll take care of it," Leanne said sharply. "Just go home."

As Leanne stomped by the greenhouse opening, she didn't even pay Bryan or Conrad any attention, but as Jack ambled by, he nodded sheepishly.

"Hey, Bryan. How are things?"

"Great, Jack. It's good to see you. Home for a visit?"

"Yeah, gotta get back to work in a day or two. The place looks great. Is everything going well?"

"It's just getting started, but it's going pretty well. Have you met Chief Harris?" Bryan held out his hand to draw Conrad over and Jack extended his hand.

"I haven't. Good to meet you, Chief. I'm Jack Summers. My mother-in-law, Mavis Bell, lives next door."

"Yes, I know Mavis," Conrad said smiling. "She's running around here somewhere."

"She's always full of energy," Jack said chuckling. "Well, I've got to get back to the house. Want to spend some time with the kids before I have to head back. Take care and good luck with the business, Bryan."

"Thanks," Bryan said waving as Jack walked away.

"Seems like a nice guy," Conrad said taking the plant back and placing it on the table.

"He is," Bryan said nodding. "I've always kind of felt sorry for him though."

§

"So, everything went okay?" Cora asked as Conrad walked up. She'd already seen Jack and they spoke briefly before he left. He seemed a bit dejected, but she hadn't noticed any anger.

"Yeah, she yelled at him, but he took it. It seems like that's their way," Conrad smirked and reached for the flat of tomatoes. "Can you ring these up for me, Amanda?"

"Sure, Chief," Amanda said as she walked behind the table they were using for outside sales. "Did you decide against getting the tomato cages?"

"Um, well," Conrad said clearing his throat. "Since I don't even know exactly what those are, I decided I'd let Georgia take care of that."

Amanda laughed and Cora slapped his arm teasingly. "Silly, it's those things you stick in the ground to support the plants when they start to get tall."

"These have a way to go before they need all that," Conrad said smiling.

"True," Cora conceded as Conrad handed a credit card to Amanda.

"You have Georgia's credit card?" Cora blurted

out when she saw it pass between them. The credit card was an eye-catching vivid blue and had butterflies all over it.

"Yes. She gave it to me when she asked me to pick these up."

Cora raised both eyebrows as Amanda giggled.

"What?" Conrad said straightening his shoulders. "I'm the Chief of Police. I guess she thinks I can be trusted."

"I guess so," Cora said chuckling as Conrad smiled.

"Are you guys leaving so soon?" Mavis Bell walked up to the table carrying a price tag gun.

"Yes, gotta get these little fellers to Georgia before they die in my hands," Conrad said holding up the flat of tomato plants. "I have that kind of special touch with plants."

"Oh, I thought you had decided to start a garden, Chief," Mavis said smiling.

"No, I've not crossed over that line yet." Conrad pushed the receipt in his shirt pocket as a customer called to Amanda.

"Oh, Chief," Mavis said rolling her eyes and smiling.

"I did have one thing I forgot to ask you earlier, Mavis," Conrad said with a wrinkled brow. "Do you know a Stanton Bell? Does that name sound familiar to you?"

Cora's eyebrows popped up in surprise and she turned to Mavis.

"No. I can't say that I do."

"Well he used to own all the land out in these parts, and I thought maybe he was a relative of Howard's."

"Might be," Mavis said tilting her head. "He did tell me his family owned all this area back in the day. I don't remember the name Stanton though. You might ask Miriam Landry. She could probably tell you."

"Hmm," Conrad said nodding and noticed Cora turning her head probably to hide her reaction. "Okay. Well, thanks Mavis. You take care. We'll see you later."

Everyone said their goodbyes as they strolled towards the parking lot.

"So, are you going to give old Miriam a call?" Cora said sarcastically.

"No, I think I'll pass on that," Conrad said haughtily as Cora giggled.

§

Cora saw Georgia's eyes light up as soon as they walked in the police department. Sitting in the dispatch office that was partially encased in glass, Georgia popped up from her seat and looked over the console through the glass to see Conrad carrying the tomato plants. Walking into Georgia's cubicle, Conrad sat the plants on the side of the counter. "There you go."

"Oh, Chief. They look great. Thank you," Georgia said as she leaned over to sniff the plants.

"Are they supposed to stink like that," Conrad scrunched his nose. "They stunk up my whole car."

Cora shook her head behind Conrad to let Georgia know he was only teasing.

"They smell wonderful," Georgia insisted. "Just like they're supposed to. There's nothing better than homegrown tomatoes."

"Well, if you say so," Conrad said handing her back her credit card.

"I'll bring you some one day. You'll see," Georgia said as she turned back around to respond to a call. It was shift change and the officers were reporting in. Georgia reached out and put her hand on Conrad's wrist as he started to walk off, holding up a finger for him to wait.

"Here, Chief," Georgia said handing him a phone message when she completed her radio call. "The coroner called while you were en route, and I told her you'd be here in a few minutes."

"Oh, okay," Conrad said glancing at Cora. "I'll give her a call back."

Walking out of dispatch, Conrad spoke quietly to Cora. "Let's go in my office and see what Alice wants before we go to lunch."

Grabbing up the phone, as they walked in the office, Conrad punched in the number on his message. Cora closed the office door and took a chair across from his desk.

"This is Chief Harris from Spicetown. I'm

returning a call to the coroner."

Conrad sat down at his desk and glanced at Cora.

"Okay, I'll be here for a little bit. Thanks." Conrad hung up the phone. "She's on another call," he said to Cora. "She's going to call back in a few minutes."

"Did you ever get that DNA from Miriam's sister?"

"I did. Her local PD sent it in, and Alice let me know she got it."

"Do you think that's what she's calling about? Maybe she has an ID."

"Could be," Conrad said fiddling with paper clips on his desk. "She asked me for contact information for Wanda last time we talked. I think she was going to call her."

"Have you been updating the Sheriff's office on all this?"

"No. The case actually belongs to Alice right now and I don't think Bobby wants to be involved in anything to do with Howard. That's probably best."

"Bobby doesn't know Howard though, right?"

"No, he says not, but Karen Goldman said they were distant cousins she'd heard, so they may be related. It's best for him to stay out of it just for appearances--" Cora jumped when the phone rang.

"Chief Harris," Conrad said when he picked up the phone.

Cora twisted in her chair in anticipation while Conrad moaned, hummed, and said okay a dozen times. He wasn't giving anything away.

"I just did today, but I haven't written it up," Conrad said nodding to Cora. "I'll get it to you Monday morning. Thanks, Alice."

Conrad released an audible sigh as Cora's gaze drilled holes in him.

"We can go to lunch now," Conrad said nonchalantly as Cora's indignation welled up. She was about to come across the desk at him and he enjoyed teasing her.

Cora stood up and slammed both of her fists into the sides of her waist to lean forward. Conrad put up both hands in defense laughing. "Okay. Okay. Take it easy."

Cora dropped back into the chair. "Spill it, Connie."

"She's got an ID and it is Howard Bell," Conrad said pressing his lips together. "She's declaring cause of death to be a blunt force trauma to the head, but she's not ready to make a call on the manner of death yet."

"Well, it's not likely suicide."

"No, but it could be accidental," Conrad offered.

"Well, he didn't plant himself in the darn ground," Cora said rising to her feet. "Something hinky was sure going on. If it was an accident, someone would have reported it, not covered it up."

Conrad fought the urge to tell Cora to simmer down because he'd learned that retort had a ricochet affect. He just nodded in agreement instead.

"Let's go get lunch and I'll come back this afternoon and write up my report with Mavis while it's fresh on my mind."

"Did you learn anything from her?"

"She has a good recall of that day," Conrad said standing and hitching up his pants. "Sounds like she's replayed it in her mind many times, but she was at work. I don't think she knows what happened. She still believes he's coming home one day."

"Who is going to tell her?"

"We are, but not just yet," Conrad said motioning Cora to join him as he opened his office door. Waving to Georgia as they headed down the hallway and out the side door, Conrad felt his phone vibrate and glanced at the text.

"So, where do you want to eat?"

CHAPTER 19

"Okay," Cora Mae said as she picked up their lunch remains and cleaned up the table.

Conrad had picked up sandwiches at Sesame Subs and they had taken them to Cora's house to eat so they could talk freely. They couldn't risk being overheard as Conrad filled her in on his call from the coroner.

"At 2:00 Alice and a deputy are going to visit Miriam while somebody with the local police is going to see Wanda, right?"

"Yes," Conrad confirmed. "And we are going to Mavis' house. Hopefully, the kids will be there, too."

"Okay. I've never done a death notification before so tell me what to expect."

"I wish I could, but no two are the same."

"What do I need to do?" Cora said slipping her sweater on and looking around for her purse.

"Just provide comfort. I'll do all the talking, but it's always best for there to be two people. She'll need a friendly face."

"Okay," Cora said breathing deeply. "Let's go."

The car ride north of town was somber, but Cora's mind was not still. "I just can't logically create any circumstance that would make me feel like I needed to bury a body I found, unless I had killed them," Cora said shaking her head. "How could this be any kind of accident?"

Conrad shrugged. "It has happened. There's a lot of emotion around death. People feel guilt from accidents and can try to cover them up sometimes. It was almost nineteen years ago when Howard disappeared. Who knows what was going on back then?"

"I guess Bing should have looked harder," Cora said shaking her head and looking down at her hands. "I'm sure Miriam reported it to him or someone that worked for him. He just thought he'd left town."

"No, actually Miriam contacted the county sheriff's department. The deputy that took the report doesn't work there anymore, but I read the report."

"Did she think someone killed him?"

"No, it just read like a missing person's report. She said he had disappeared, and no one knew where he was. She made allegations he was not of sound mind, might have wandered off, that kind of thing. There wasn't any mention of suspicion someone had done anything to him."

"Not of sound mind," Cora screeched. "I've never heard anything like that. Why would she say something like that?"

"I don't know. The medical reports I've seen don't support that either."

"When did Howard's mother die again?"

"1997, I think."

"Was there an estate or anything filed?" Cora turned in her seat to stare at the side of Conrad's head while he drove.

"I don't know," Conrad said quizzically. "But I'm going to check on that first thing Monday."

"Maybe she was part owner of all this land? We need to find out who Stanton is. Did you ask Wanda?"

"No, but I can," Conrad said. "She didn't seem very connected to the family though. I got the feeling she left town young and stayed away. I'll need to give it a few days before I contact her."

"Yes, she needs time to process the information."

"I didn't ask Miriam either, but that whole interview wasn't very productive and frankly, I don't think Miriam would tell me even if she knew."

"Uncooperative, was she?" Cora said smiling. "I've never known her to be any other way."

Conrad chuckled as they drove past Stotlar's Nursery for the second time that day. "I'm going to check the house first. If she's not there, we'll have to go back to Bryan's and get her."

"I think Amanda told me Mavis just helps out in the mornings, so she should be home by now. I don't know about Leanne though."

Pulling into Mavis' gravel driveway, they saw her outside in a small garden off on the edge of the side lawn. Mavis turned around and waved to them as she brushed off her hands.

"Well, hello you two," Mavis called out cheerily as she approached.

"Hello, Mavis," Conrad said. "You just can't get enough gardening?"

"Well, all of Bryan's stuff gets me inspired," Mavis chuckled. "I had to put out a few things of my own."

"Can we come inside?" Conrad said holding out his arm to motion her towards the door. "I need to talk to you for a minute."

"Sure, Chief. Come on in. Leanne's still over at Bryan's, but Daniel is inside."

Holding the door open, Conrad followed Cora inside and glanced around. Daniel was sitting on the couch with the remote in his hand and he nodded hello.

"Can I get you both something to drink? Iced Tea?"

"Oh, no," Conrad said. "No, thank you. We'll just be a minute. Are your grandchildren here?"

"They're out back playing. Come on in. Have a seat." Mavis tapped her son on the arm and Daniel moved over so she could sit. Conrad and Cora took chairs across the room.

"Mavis, I've got some bad news I need to tell you," Conrad said beginning slowly.

"Bad news?" Mavis said squinting her eyes and Cora could see she was searching her mind for what it could be.

"The coroner called me this afternoon and they've identified the bones Bryan found. They do belong to Howard."

The few seconds of silence were fragile, and Cora realized she needed to let herself breathe as she tried to focus on Mavis. Flashbacks of doctors coming to tell Cora that Bing had died were choking out her thoughts and clouding her reaction. "I'm so sorry, Mavis," Cora said clutching at the ribbing on the bottom of her sweater and fighting back tears from her own painful memories.

"No, that can't be," Mavis said as her son scooted closer and put a protective arm around her. "That can't be Howard. How could he, how did he get there? How did he die?"

"The coroner says he died from a head trauma, but they don't know anything else yet. It could have been an accident or—"

"But he didn't bury himself," Mavis said indignantly even though tears began to fall. "Nobody would want to kill Howard. Why did this happen? Are they sure? Did they have DNA?"

"Yes, they compared DNA from his sister," Conrad said as Cora handed Mavis a tissue from a small box she had shoved in her purse before they left home.

"Miriam?"

"No, his sister, Wanda," Conrad said softly. Cora pulled out another tissue and dabbed at her own eyes.

"I can't imagine how this can be," Mavis said becoming more composed. "What happens now? They need to find out who did this."

"You need to decide what you want to do next. The coroner will call you in a couple of days. They will want to know where to release the body to, a funeral home or a crematorium. It will be something you will need to decide as next of kin."

"Have you told Miriam?"

"I haven't, but the coroner is talking to her now."

"She'll want him cremated and I don't want that," Mavis said chewing on her bottom lip and sniffing.

"Legally, it is your decision to make right now. Whether you want to discuss it with Howard's family is up to you, but the coroner will contact you for those arrangements."

"Are they going to try to find out what really happened? Is somebody going to find out who killed him?"

"The coroner's office is still working on it. If they find evidence, they'll turn all that over to the sheriff's department," Conrad said as he stood. "I'm sorry, Mavis. Truly, I am."

Cora stood and left the tissue box on the table. Mavis rose to walk them to the door and hugged Cora tightly bringing fresh tears to both of their eyes. "You call me if I can help you," Cora said wiping a tear from Mavis' cheek with her thumb. "If I can help you at all, please let me know."

"I will. Thank you, Cora Mae. And thank you, Chief. I know, I know this isn't fun for you either. I'm sorry I'm such a mess," Mavis said wiping at her eyes.

"I'll be by Monday to check on you," Conrad said patting Mavis' shoulder. Mavis nodded as she slowly closed the door.

§

"Thank you for coming with me," Conrad said as they backed out of the driveway. "I know that wasn't easy for you, but I think it helped Mavis to have you there instead of another police officer."

"Oh, I was happy I could help. I'm not very good at it, but I hope it helped her. It's a horrible thing. A truly horrible thing to live through." Cora had lost Bing many years ago, but Conrad remembered how lost she had been right after it happened. There was a vacant look in her eyes as if life was moving around her and she wasn't participating. She did bounce back, but it took several weeks. He hadn't thought about how hard this would be for her when he had asked her to accompany him.

"I think she was grateful."

"Although this is horrible news, at least she has already grown accustomed to his absence. I think that is what hit me harder than anything. Having an empty house, feeling like you lost half of yourself. Having her kids there will help, too. I felt so alone," Cora said looking down at her hands in her lap. "It's something you never forget."

Conrad nodded and they drove in silence.

Coasting into town and driving slowly down Fennel Street, Conrad surveyed the businesses and sidewalk traffic. "I'm going to drop you off at home and go back to the office so I can write up all this for Alice."

Cora shifted to her hip and frowned at Conrad. "What about insurance? Howard would have life insurance, wouldn't he?"

"He was a miner," Conrad said shrugging and glancing over at Cora. "Don't they have good benefits?"

"But his mine closed. Maybe that insurance is only for work-related accidents."

"That could be," Conrad said. "I can check on that Monday."

"I asked Amanda to check on Mavis' property to see what name the deed was in and then I forgot to ask her what she found," Cora said slapping her leg. "I'll do that Monday."

"It could be Stanton Bell if it's a family home."

"Didn't you think it was odd Mavis popped up with that comment about Miriam wanting him cremated?"

"It did stand out to me," Conrad said as he slowed for a stop sign. "Maybe it's a religious issue for her."

"Or maybe it's come up in the family before," Cora said pointing at Conrad. "I wonder how their mother's death was handled. Maybe Miriam fought to have her cremated, too."

"Could be. I can ask Wanda if she knows anything about it when I call her on the Stanton Bell issue."

"And Daniel," Cora paused and frowned. "He didn't say a single word. I mean he put his arm around Mavis, but he didn't react at all."

"Not at all," Conrad agreed. He had noticed that as well. "Don't read too much into it, though," Conrad said as he turned the car into Cora's driveway. "People are not rational or normal when they get news like this and everybody reacts differently. Some people are very stoic and seem cold, but they fall apart later. It's a process and everybody is different."

"I thought Mavis reacted pretty much like I expected," Cora said. "She was shocked, sad, indignant, then questioning. It seemed like a normal progression of feelings to me."

"Yes, but I've had people take a swing at me when I had to tell them they lost a loved one. Sometimes they lash out, scream or crumple to the ground. It's all over the place. You can't predict much from a situation like that."

"Everyone has to find their own coping skills," Cora said as she released her seatbelt.

"Some go right back to work, and others can't get out of bed," Conrad added. "Neither one is any indication of their involvement. It's just who they are."

Cora opened the car door and put one foot on the ground before pulling her purse from the floorboard. "I can tell you who Daniel is," Cora said looking over her shoulder. "He's a dark, disturbed young man. He always has been."

Cora pushed herself out of the car with a groan. She felt exhausted from the internal tension of the day. "Call me if you hear anything."

"I will," Conrad said as Cora shut the door.

CHAPTER 20

Conrad shuffled slowly into the police department's side door. He really didn't feel like writing reports but had too much on his mind to go home. Just as he was about to secretly make another of Cora's lists, Georgia appeared at his door.

"I didn't think you were coming back in today."

"I wasn't but I have a few things that shouldn't really wait. I don't plan to be here long. Everything okay?"

"Miriam Landry called and wants you to call her back."

Conrad was too tired to hold in the dismay he felt and groaned as Georgia giggled.

"Good news is, I told her you wouldn't be back in until Monday, so she's not expecting a call today."

"That does help," Conrad said chuckling. "Thank you."

"Anytime, Chief."

"Can you pull my door closed for me?"

"Sure," Georgia said reaching in to grab the door knob. "See you Monday."

Conrad pulled his notebook from his desk and began to copy his notes from Mavis' interview at Bryan's, adding all the detail he could recall. He would type it up formally on Monday and send it to Alice, but his notes were sparse, and he didn't want to forget the small things. He had decided Daniel and Leanne needed to be interviewed based on the relationship issues Mavis mentioned, but today was not the day for it. He should probably wait until the funeral is held if that is what Mavis was planning.

Next, he made a list of things he had promised Cora he would do Monday, including issues he wanted to talk with Wanda about. She had seemed fairly detached about Howard's disappearance when he had spoken to her earlier. Not uncaring, but definitely disconnected to her family's life here in Spicetown. She seemed sincere in her interest to help and Conrad felt confident she would not feel affronted by his questions.

Carmen Maddox was still unchecked on his list, too. He was not eager to talk to her and had hoped to avoid it if possible. Now that they were looking at a crime, it was going to be necessary. Andrew Gentry had been located by Officer Tabor and

Conrad thought he would call him before reaching out to Carmen. The more he knew before talking to Carmen, the better off he thought he would be.

Dixie Martin's mother and Cora's neighbor might have something useful to share too but seeing Jack Summers cower to Leanne today had planted a seed in his mind. Jack would do anything Leanne told him to, but to what length would he keep that secret?

After drafting some interview questions for each person on his list, he researched the mine closure on the Internet and jotted down some phone numbers to call Monday. Shutting down his computer, he sneaked out the side door without any goodbyes and hoped the city had a peaceful Saturday night.

§

"Well, that's just great," Cora muttered to herself when she opened her front door to grab the Sunday paper. The front-page headline read *"Bones Identified as Local Man"*. Snatching up the paper, she took it back to the kitchen to get coffee. She hadn't even thought about the newspaper announcing all of this. Her mind had been whirling all night on whether one of her beloved Spicetown citizens was a murderer and if so, which one. For a man no one seemed to hate, there were a number of possibilities.

"Marmalade," Cora said stooping down to put food in her bowl. "What is the world coming to?" Putting the food back in the pantry, Cora jumped when the doorbell sounded. Looking down at her tattered housecoat, she shrugged and decided the visitor deserved no better at this hour in the morning.

"Good morning," Cora said when she opened the door to her nervous neighbor, Sandy Nash.

"So sorry to bother you, Mayor, but I saw you had picked up your paper. Can I come in?"

"Certainly," Cora said opening the door wider and forcing a pleasant smile. "I haven't had a chance to read the paper yet, Sandy. Is there something in it that troubles you?"

"Oh, I'm sorry, but yes. They identified those bones."

"Ah, yes," Cora said calmly. "Would you like some coffee?"

"No, thank you," Sandy said standing awkwardly in the kitchen waiting for Cora to pour some for herself.

"Have a seat," Cora said waving her to the kitchen table. "Now, let me see what it says," Cora said opening up the newspaper with a snap.

"It says they know the bones belong to Howard Bell. He's the guy I told you my friend, Dixie, was dating. Do you think they're sure? I mean, where's Dixie if he's dead?"

Cora tried to read through Sandy's babble but

could only scan it enough to see it implied wrongdoing. She was hoping they would stick to the facts, but it must have been too tempting to ignore speculation.

"Well, I can tell you that yes, they are sure it is Howard, but I don't know what happened to your friend."

"What if she's buried somewhere up there too?"

"They removed a large portion of the area and used ground penetrating radar to see if there was anything else there. They didn't find anything. I'm sorry about your friend, but I don't think she's buried out there."

Sandy just looked down at the edge of the table. "I don't know what to do. I can't believe someone can just vanish and there's nothing that can be done."

"Well, has her mother hired an investigator or had anyone do a search for her? It's always possible she left town and didn't want to be found."

"I still feel like she would have let me know."

"She might not have wanted to put you in the middle, put you in a bad spot because you knew, especially thinking her mom would contact you."

"My husband, Marty, told me not to get my hopes up," Sandy said sadly. "It's just something I can't shake. I still think about her after all these years."

"Did you know when she saw Howard last? I mean were you aware of when they met or were together?"

"Sometimes," Sandy said raising her head. "I mean she'd talk about him the next day. She'd say they had met somewhere the night before."

"When did you see Dixie last?"

"A week before Christmas," Sandy said. "She was planning to spend Christmas Eve with him, and she talked about the gift she'd bought. She showed it to me. It was a watch."

"So, you saw her on the 18th?"

"I think so. I've got it written down at home and I'd have to check to be sure."

"I believe Howard disappeared before that, so…"

"But whoever killed him, could have killed Dixie too, and just put her somewhere else."

"There are a lot of possibilities," Cora said as she stood to start making herself some breakfast. "I'll tell the Chief about your concerns though."

"Thank you," Sandy said standing. "I'm sorry to bother you again. I just thought the headlines meant maybe there was a chance she…"

"I know, dear," Cora said patting her shoulder as she led her to the door.

CHAPTER 21

"Connie, what are you doing right now?" Cora yelled through the phone as soon as Conrad answered.

"I'm watching the game," Conrad said. "What's wrong?"

"I need you. Can you leave right now?" Cora was squirming in the seat of her car. "Talk faster. This is urgent."

"Yes. Yeah, let me get my shoes on. Where are you?" Conrad jumped up and hit the speaker button to free his hands so he could hurriedly tie his shoes. "What's wrong?"

"I'm on the north road about 50 yards south of the nursery. I need you to go to Mavis' house right now."

"Why are you sitting south of the nursery? Are you in your car?"

"I'll explain while you're driving. Don't stop to talk. Keep moving."

"Cora, this is crazy. Are you in some kind of danger? I might have a car in the area."

"Hurry up," Cora felt her phone vibrate that another call was coming in. "I'll call you back."

Conrad flew out the front door with his keys in his hands and set up the Bluetooth in the car to call back Cora as soon as he started backing out of his driveway.

"Mavis, are you all right?" Cora said when she switched over to her second call.

"Are you coming, Cora? She's having a fit." Cora could hear screaming in the background telling Mavis to hang up the phone.

"Yes, I'm on my way and the Chief's coming, too."

"Thank you," Mavis whispered before disconnecting.

Looking down at her phone that would not be still, she pushed the button to answer Conrad's return call.

"Cora," he shouted. "What's going on?"

"Are you on your way?" Cora got out of her car and slammed the door.

"Yes, I'm going down Fennel Street now. Are you all right? What's happened?"

"Miriam is on a rage. She's down at Mavis' house screaming at her. Mavis needs help but she wouldn't call you."

"Are you at Mavis' house now?"

"No, I'm still just south of Bryan's, but I'm walking toward the nursery now. Don't worry about me. Mavis just called again, and she needs you."

"I'm turning on the road now. Why are you walking?"

"I have a flat tire. Mavis is panicked and I knew she couldn't wait for me to walk up that hill."

"I'll stop and pick you up." Conrad rounded the bend in the road and could see her car on the side of the road.

"No, just go to her. I'll get Bryan to help me. I don't want Mavis to wait any longer."

"Okay, I'll come back for you once I get Miriam out of there," Conrad said as he passed Cora on the road and waved.

Pulling his car up next to Miriam's, he got out and walked quickly to the door. He could hear Miriam shouting even through the closed door. Opening the screen door, he knocked loudly on the door and was relieved when the shouting stopped.

"Chief," Mavis said meekly. "How nice to see you."

"Hi, Mavis. Can I come in? I just came by to check on you," Conrad said as Mavis pulled the door open wider. "Oh, hello Miriam. I didn't expect you to be here. How nice," Conrad said through gritted teeth.

"I don't want to be here either," Miriam said lashing out at them both. "But somebody has to talk some sense into this woman."

"I can't imagine what you are talking about, Miriam," Conrad said. Mavis looked demurely at the Chief, clearly relieved to have someone on her side.

"You shouldn't be wasting your time visiting anyone. You should be finding out what happened to my brother. Somebody needs to be held accountable and she had to have something to do with it." Miriam's arm was fully extended to point directly at Mavis.

"So, you think Mavis killed her own husband, do you? And why would she do that?"

"Because he was cheating on her," Miriam shouted. "Everybody in town knew it. He was humiliating her. She'd rather have the insurance money than be a laughingstock. She did something to him and you aren't doing anything about it."

"You don't get insurance money for a man that disappears," Conrad said calmly. "If that's what she wanted, she wouldn't have waited almost twenty years for someone to find him."

"I'm sure she thought the local police might look for him and then she could claim it when he was found. She didn't realize nobody did anything at all. They didn't even investigate."

"Actually, I read the report you filed. You didn't give any indication you thought your brother had come to any harm or that anyone else was involved in his disappearance. You suggested he had mental problems and might have wandered off. I found that very suspicious since there is no medical evidence to support any of those allegations. In fact, there aren't even idle town rumors to that effect, so it seems rather odd you are now accusing Mavis of wrongdoing. You know, falsifying a police report--"

"Don't you preach at me, Conrad Harris. I did it because she wouldn't, and somebody had to report it. Howard lived here his whole life and then one day he just disappears. Somebody had to do something, so I took that responsibility into my own hands. I hadn't even talked to Howard in years, so I told that deputy maybe it happened because he was touched in the head. I didn't know where he was."

Mavis walked away and sat quietly on the couch as Conrad took her place in front of Miriam. "Miriam, exactly why are you here?"

"We have things that have to be worked out, family things. It's no concern of yours."

"I don't think that's entirely true," Conrad said looking at Mavis. "I think Mavis would like me to be involved, so please, tell me what your concerns are. Is it something to do with Howard's funeral?"

"No," Miriam said with a dismissive wave of her hand. "The coroner already told me I didn't have any say in that and she doesn't care what I want."

"Then what are the matters that need to be discussed?"

"I'm not talking to you," Miriam said grabbing at her purse she had tossed into an arm chair.

"Well, we don't have to talk right now," Conrad said slowly, trying to delay Miriam's exit. "But with an open investigation and possibly an inquest, you may have to talk to me, eventually."

"I don't have to talk to you, Conrad," Miriam said in a huff as she reached for the doorknob.

"You can always speak with the Attorney General's office or the Ohio Bureau of Criminal Investigation if you'd prefer. BCI has an open case on your brother's death now as well."

"I'll talk to the Sheriff about this," Miriam bristled.

"I don't think your cousin can help you with these matters." Miriam scowled and grabbed to pull the door open. Struggling to get the latch to release, Conrad thought sure he saw steam come from her ears.

Only when the door slammed shut did Mavis' shoulders relax.

"I'm so sorry, Chief. I didn't want to drag you out here on a Sunday. I talked to Cora--"

"Yes, she told me. She's down at Bryan's house now. She had a flat tire and couldn't get to you, so she called me."

"I'm really sorry but I've never been able to deal with Miriam when she's angry."

"Few can," Conrad chuckled. "Frankly, I think this all worked out for the best. Cora would have just been yelling back at her and she could have future consequences from that. It's best that it was me. I don't have to work with Miriam like Cora does."

"She is so unruly, I swear," Mavis said shaking her head. "I've never been able to work out anything with her. She always screamed at Howard, too. He just couldn't take her anymore either and that's why we quit going to dinner at his mom's on Sunday. He started just stopping in through the week so he could check on his mom without seeing Miriam. She's a hard lady."

"Hard headed," Conrad agreed. "Well, let me get going. Cora's car needs to get fixed and I'll check on you tomorrow. Okay?"

"Okay, Chief. Thank you again and thank Cora for me, too."

"I will."

When Conrad pulled up to Cora's car, he saw Bryan already had the wheel off and Bryan told him he didn't need any help, so he drove up to the nursery to find her. The sun was setting, and the air was cooler. He saw Cora standing near the parking lot entrance with her arms wrapped around her.

"Hop in and I'll take you down to the car. Bryan's almost done."

"Is Mavis okay? I saw Miriam fly by in a rage. That woman is going to die young with all that anger inside her."

"Well, she sure doesn't keep anything in," Conrad said chuckling. "At least she turned on me when I got there and gave Mavis a break. I can't promise she won't try it again though. There's something she wants to discuss with Mavis, something very important to her and she won't tell me what it is."

"Do you think it's about the burial?"

"No, I don't think so," Conrad said. "She said it was a family matter, but unless Howard had something she wanted... I don't know. I didn't think Howard had any assets or anything. I don't know what it could be. I'm going to call on Mavis again tomorrow when she's had a chance to breathe and ask her. Maybe she'll tell me."

"I'll get Amanda digging around first thing in the morning. Are you interviewing tomorrow?"

"Yeah, I've got several people to talk to," Conrad said feeling anxious to get started yet also dreading it at the same time.

"Did you make a list?" Cora said arching her eyebrows high. Cora was a famous list maker and she always nagged at Conrad to embrace her organizational skills. Although he privately found lists very helpful, he preferred to tease her about the time she wasted making hers.

"I got it all up here," Conrad said tapping his index finger on his temple while Cora laughed.

CHAPTER 22

"Morning, Chief," Georgia called out when she saw Conrad come in the side door stomping his feet. The weather had turned back to spring showers during the night and rain was lashing down now. Shaking his coat out in the hallway and tipping his head over before removing his hat, a puddle had formed at his feet.

"Lousy weather," Conrad said as his shoes squeaked down on the linoleum. "Everything okay so far?" Rain this hard sometimes meant a few collisions in town between those that pulled over and those that pushed through the hard rains.

"Just one call and Tabor is handling it. I've got a phone message for you, too," Georgia said as Conrad approached the dispatch office. "Sorry, Chief. The Sheriff wants you to call him."

"Okay," Conrad said without surprise. He

expected Bobby to be frustrated the case had broken in a way he couldn't directly be involved.

"I guess it's about the bones. Did you do the death notification?"

"Yes, I talked to Mavis, but the coroner told Miriam." Conrad headed back to his office.

"Well, you got the better end of that," Georgia called out behind him as Conrad shut his office door.

How sad it must be when no one wants to talk to you. He wondered why Miriam had to treat people so badly. She was a bright, capable woman and despite their disagreements on the vision for the city of Spicetown, she did some good things for the town as the president of the Chamber of Commerce, yet she didn't have a single friend.

"Chief Harris, returning the Sheriff's call," Conrad said when the phone was answered. Bobby Bell never answered his own phone.

"Connie," Bobby said quietly when he answered the phone. "Rough weekend."

"Yes, for some," Conrad said, surprised at Bobby's passive greeting. Today was going to be gloomy on every level.

"You've started interviews?"

"I have. I have several more planned today." Conrad pulled out his secret to-do list and numbered them in the order he planned to call. "I've got some contact information—"

"Don't tell me any details," Bobby interrupted. "I need to stay away from all this so I'm leaving it in your hands."

"That's fine."

"If you need help, we'll pull in the State, but I don't want my name tied to this. I don't know Howard Bell, but he is related to me somehow, I'm told. I don't need there to be any appearances of impropriety."

"I understand."

"I want you to keep Alice updated though and she'll coordinate everything with the county prosecutor if it comes to that."

"Will do."

"Oh, and Connie," Bobby said in closing, "Don't mess this up."

Before Conrad could reassure him he would do his best, Bobby Bell had hung up on him again.

§

"Oh, Amanda," Cora called out when she heard a noise in the outer office. "Is that you?"

"Yes, Mayor. I'm here," Amanda said looking in Cora's doorway. "You're in the office early today."

"Yes, much to do," Cora said standing up and walking around her desk. "Looks like you took a bath on the way in today." Cora chuckled as Amanda peeled off her rain jacket and propped her umbrella in the corner of the room.

"Ugh, my hair is ruined. I don't know why I bothered."

"It is so dark out there now. It was just beginning to sprinkle when I came in, but it's hitting the windows pretty hard now."

"And it's Monday," Amanda moaned.

"I bet you're tired working all weekend at the nursery and then coming in here all week. You're going to have to find some time for yourself somewhere or it's going to get to be too much."

"It's just for the start. When things get going well, Bryan will be able to afford to hire people. Then maybe we'll have some time to do fun stuff."

"I hate to tell you this, but I think he's going to be working around the clock all summer. If he's going to do landscaping as well as run the nursery, it's going to be longer than you think. Having your own business can really swallow up your life, especially at the start. I hope you both can hang in there. He seems to be doing really well. You got him off to a great start."

"I hope so," Amanda said wistfully. "So, what brought you to work so early? Did you know it was going to pour down rain?"

"I didn't sleep well, and I was up earlier than usual. I just thought I'd get started. Go ahead and get your computer up. I need you to look up Mavis' property. We talked about it last week but then I forgot about it. I need to know who owns it."

"Oh, I looked it up. I guess I forgot to tell you. It's owned by that same LLC, Stanton Bell." Amanda entered her password and stared at her monitor. "It has been for years."

"I thought that might be the case. We need to know what this LLC is about. Can you pull a list of all the property they currently own in the county?"

"I think so," Amanda said. "We may have to get a plat map to figure out where it is if it's out in the county. There won't be a street address or anything."

"Is that online too?"

"Probably. Let me look."

"Oh, and one more thing," Cora said turning towards her office door. "Pull up any property owned by Miriam Landry and see who deeded it to her."

"Okay," Amanda said as Cora went into her office and shut the door. It was time to reach into the history of Spicetown and call her friend and mentor, Violet Hoenigberg. Miss Violet knew all the old gossip in town.

§

Having failed to connect with Miriam's sister, Wanda, Conrad moved to the next person on his list. Officer Tabor had located Carmen's ex-husband in West Virginia. He had opened a store there and Conrad felt certain he would be easier to talk to than Carmen Maddox. He kept cautiously moving Carmen further down every time he renumbered his list.

"Gentry Tires."

"Good morning. I'm trying to reach Andrew Gentry."

"This is Andrew. How can I help you?"

"This is Conrad Harris. I'm the Chief of Police in Spicetown, Ohio. Do you have a few minutes to speak with me?"

"Sure. How can I help you?"

"I don't know if you keep up on the news around Spicetown anymore—"

"No, Chief," Andrew said chuckling. "I haven't been back to Spicetown in over ten years."

"Well, recently there was body discovered that has been identified as Howard Bell. Did you know Howard?"

"No, not personally, but I knew of him."

"That's kind of why I'm calling," Conrad said. "Your name was linked to him because of Carmen and I wanted to ask a few questions about that."

"Look, Chief. I don't know the man at all. Carmen's name was linked to everybody. That was part of the problem in our marriage," Andrew said.

"I'm trying to discern what is gossip and what is truth," Conrad explained. "Do you have any direct knowledge that Howard Bell was in a relationship with your ex-wife? I mean did you ever see them together or talk to him at all?"

"Never," Andrew stated flatly. "Just gossip. For all I knew, she spread it. I think she thought it would make me jealous and she caused a lot of it herself. Have you talked to her yet?"

"No, not yet."

"She's crazy, Chief. You can't believe anything she says. She has documented mental health issues."

"Well, that's one of the reasons I'm calling you first. I don't need to deal in gossip right now. I wanted to know if there was anything valid in the stories that she was in a relationship with Howard or pregnant with his child when your marriage ended. Howard Bell is mentioned in your divorce and that caused me some concern. Were you alleging—"

"No, Chief. I didn't really think he was seeing Carmen. I thought she started those rumors and I was going to use them against her. I can't help you with your investigation and I don't think she can either."

"Okay," Conrad said. "I appreciate your candor. If I need a signed statement from you at some point, would you have any reservations about supplying that?"

"Not at all. Whatever you need, just let me know."

Conrad thanked him and ended his call with a sigh of relief. Perhaps nothing further would be needed from Carmen.

§

"Okay, I've got some things together for you here," Amanda said walking around Cora's desk with a stack of papers. "This is a current list of holdings. Stanton Bell LLC owns seventeen properties right now."

"Wow," Cora said jerking her head back. "That's a lot. Why have I never heard of this LLC before?"

"Well, probably because it's mostly farmland. There are only three houses here in town that show up as being owned by the LLC."

"Is one of them Miriam's?" Cora looked up expectantly at Amanda.

"No, her house is in her name."

"Who did she buy it from?"

"She didn't buy it. It was quit-claimed from Stanton Bell LLC to her in 1998," Amanda said handing Cora a copy of the deed.

"So, someone signed it over to her, because I know she lived in it before that. She's always been in the same house."

"See the signature," Amanda said pointing to the bottom of the page. "It's just the name of the Registered Agent. It still doesn't tell us who they are."

"We can find out, can't we?"

§

"Hi, Wanda," Conrad said when Georgia transferred him a call from Miriam's sister. "I'm so glad you had the chance to call back. Are you doing okay?"

"Yes. It was a shock to see the officers at my front door, but at least I was a little prepared. I hope you can find out who did this to Howard."

"Well, we are definitely going to try. It's difficult with the time lapse, but I did have one quick question for you I didn't ask earlier." Conrad was relieved she sounded strongly committed to continuing to help with the investigation.

"Certainly. I'll help any way I can."

"Have you heard of Stanton Bell, LLC? Is this someone in your family?"

"Stanton is my mother's maiden name," Wanda said tentatively. "I think this is the partnership or agreement my dad came to with my grandfather."

"So, Stanton is your mother's father and the Bell is your father?"

"Yes, they did some partnering on some property purchases and my mom's house, too. The company owned it, instead of my parents. They used to lease land to farmers and had some rentals in town. I thought all of that had been dissolved now though. When my mom died, I thought that was all sold."

"What happened to your mom's house when she passed away? Did you sell it?"

"Oh, I don't know those details. Miriam said she'd take care of it and for me not to worry. She said she'd make sure any outstanding bills were paid and she did mail me some paper to sign so I didn't have to travel back to Spicetown. It let her handle the closing or whatever she had to do for the estate. She took care of it."

"So, there wasn't any life insurance or inheritance involved?"

"Oh, no," Wanda said. "My parents lived pretty meagerly, and my mom had been sick for a while. I'm sure there were medical bills and funeral bills. Lots of little details, but nothing of value to be concerned with. Miriam is good at handling all those kinds of things. She always took care of that stuff for Mom, too. I doubt Howard even got involved."

"Was there a will, or an estate probated?"

"Hmm, I'm not sure," Wanda hesitated. "I think I remember Miriam telling me the house was in a trust, so it didn't have to be probated or something like that. She planned to sell the house and pay the remaining bills. If there was any little left, that would just go to her for her trouble. I told her I didn't expect anything, and I was just glad she was there to handle it all."

"Did you come back to Spicetown when your mom passed away? I'm assuming her services were here in town?"

"They were, but I wasn't able to come. I have some health problems and I was on dialysis when my mom passed. I couldn't really travel back then."

"Oh, I didn't realize. I'm sorry. Your health has improved since then?"

"Oh, yes," Wanda said. "I had a kidney

transplant and so far, things have gone well. I was very sick for a number of years though. I couldn't even come home to see mom before she died, but I did talk to her. She always told me not to worry, Miriam was taking care of everything for her. I'm sure Miriam can give you any details you need."

"Well, thank you for your time. I appreciate the call and this information is helpful."

"Chief," Wanda said timidly. "I know Miriam can be difficult at times. She's not very patient with people. She's not patient with me either, but she has a good heart. I know she'd want to help find out what happened to Howard."

"I hope you're right, Wanda."

CHAPTER 23

"Okay, I've got a lot here to sort out," Amanda said blowing out a puff of air to ruffle her bangs. "This may create more confusion than provide answers, but I've pulled everything I can think of."

"My goodness," Cora said standing up from her desk. "Let's take that over to the conference table where we can spread out."

"These are the deeds for the seventeen properties the LLC owns now. Most all of them are dated in the 1970s or '80s." Amanda placed one stack of her papers on the table. "This is a plat map where I tried to mark where I think they are."

"Who owned these properties before?"

"All except two were previously owned by Lawrence Stanton and he transferred them to the LLC."

"And the other two?" Cora asked.

"One is Miriam Landry's house. It was bought by the LLC from the Bank of Spicetown and the other is a house on Coriander Court. It was previously owned by Ned Carey."

"That's Conrad's coffee drinking buddy," Cora said. "He's always in the Fennel Street Bakery in the morning and Conrad has coffee with him."

"The lawyer?"

"Yes, he has an office just off Ginger Street. I don't think he ever lived on Coriander Court though," Cora said. "Who lives there now?"

"I didn't look that up. Want me to go check?"

"Yes, please do. Check and see who is paying the water bill."

§

"Mrs. Martin? This is Chief Harris from the Spicetown Police Department. I was wondering if I could ask you a few questions?"

"Oh, of course you can, Chief. I read all the news about the bones and everything. Sandy Nash told me my daughter, Dixie, knew that man that died and Sandy talked to the Mayor about it."

"Yes, she told me about speaking with Sandy. I saw the report you filed back in 1999. The report says that she had been missing since December 19."

"That's right. She didn't show up for her last shift at work at Sesame Subs before she was due to come home for Christmas."

"That's why I'm calling. Are you certain about that date? I mean, did you or someone see Dixie on December 18th of 1999?"

"Well, I didn't because she was living in Spicetown, but Sandy saw her. I think they worked together that day. Is that important?"

"Howard Bell disappeared on the 17th, so that's why I was curious. It may not mean anything. I have not seen any evidence of a connection between your daughter and Mr. Bell. I just wanted to check those dates," Conrad said marking Dixie off his list.

"I guess the restaurant could confirm that. Sandy seemed pretty sure about the date. Maybe you could talk to them and see."

"I'll check on it. Thank you, Mrs. Martin."

§

When his stomach began to growl, Conrad reached for the phone.

"Cora?"

"Aaaaah, good grief, Connie. You almost gave me a heart attack," Cora screeched into the phone. "I was just picking up the phone to call you."

"I didn't even hear it ring," Conrad said laughing. "What did you need?"

"I was going to tell you to come over if you can. Amanda has unearthed all kinds of information on this LLC and I thought you might want to see it. What did you need?"

"I was calling to see if you wanted to go to lunch."

"Well, we must both have things to share," Cora said chuckling.

"It sounds that way. Why don't I just pick up something for lunch and bring it over?"

"That sounds like a good idea. Did you talk to Carmen today?"

"No," Conrad said. "I don't think I need to now. I talked to Andrew and he seemed pretty certain Carmen had nothing to do with Howard."

"What?" Cora fell back in her chair and tossed her head back. "Are you kidding me? That talk was all over town. How could that be?"

"Andrew says she made it all up. He didn't paint the picture that Carmen was a credible interview. I don't think I could believe anything she said."

"I'd have to agree if that affair was a fabrication. She put up with a lot of negative attention from that rumor and what rational person does that when it only hurts them?"

"It probably caused her son some grief, too. I don't see the need to pursue that right now. I'm going to drive out and see Mavis again though."

"You'll want to after you see what Amanda has here."

"Okay. I'll pick up some sandwiches and be right

over."

§

"Good morning, Miss Violet," Cora said with a smile on her face. Violet Hoenigberg was Cora's mentor when she was a new fifth grade teacher at Peppermint Elementary and she remained one of her favorite people.

"Cora Mae," Violet said cheerily. "It's so nice to hear from you. What are you up to today?"

"Well, I've been digging around a little, digging up some old rumors and some old deeds. I called to pick your brain a little."

"You best get to it while I still got some brain cells left," Violet said with a schoolgirl's giggle despite her passing her eightieth birthday.

"Have you ever heard of a company called Stanton Bell, LLC?"

"Hmm, not directly, but if I were a gambler, I'd place my bet that it has something to do with Erwin Bell and Lawrence Stanton. You know Erwin married Lawrence Stanton's daughter, Nora. Lawrence Stanton was a big wheeler-dealer and Erwin was lazy. He wanted an easy ride. I always thought Erwin took advantage of Lawrence. Not that Lawrence wasn't a sharp guy, but he did whatever he could to make sure his daughter was taken care of."

"So, you think the two of them might have

formed this partnership to give Erwin some income?"

"Just speculation, but that would be my guess," Violet said. "You found deeds with that name?"

"I did. The problem is the LLC still owns property around the county and both men are gone now."

"I read about the bones. I'm sure you're digging around in that, aren't you?"

"Yes, a little," Cora admitted. "You know I'm nosy."

"Yes, a little." Violet laughed. "What rumors have stirred up?"

"There was a lot of talk back around the time Howard Bell disappeared that he might be involved with Carmen Maddox. Conrad doesn't seem to think those rumors are accurate."

"I think he's right to doubt anything linked to Carmen Gentry or whatever her name is now. The girl is troubled. Howard Bell was a good man from what I knew. I don't know why she went after him."

"He wasn't the only one," Cora muttered under her breath.

"So, who owns the property now?"

"I don't know. We'll have to find out who Stanton Bell LLC belongs to first. It's all still in that company name."

"Well, the LLC could have been sold or it could be that it all passed to the kids. Howard might have owned it."

"Yes, I thought Erwin might have wanted it to go that way since he was his only son," Cora said. That generation did favor the sons when it came to business.

"But you know Howard," Violet said hesitating. "He wasn't the, well, he wasn't really business minded."

"Yes, that's true. I'll keep digging."

"Well, good luck, honey. Don't get yourself in trouble snooping around now."

§

"Sorry, I'm late," Conrad called out as he came through Cora's office door with lunch bags. "I ran into Ned Carey down at the sub shop and we got to talkin'."

"I've seen that happen," Cora said smirking as she reached for one of the bags Conrad placed on the table.

"Where's Amanda?"

"She just left with Bryan. They're walking downtown for lunch."

"So, what did she dig up?" Conrad spread out the wrapper from his foot-long sub and took a huge bite.

"First, she pulled all the deeds for the properties held by Stanton Bell, LLC. They are in that stack, but here is the map showing where the properties can be found."

Conrad frowned at the map while he chewed, and Cora spread out her sandwich wrapper. "Umm," Conrad hummed as he tapped his finger on Howard Bell's property.

"Yes," Cora acknowledged Conrad's interest. "That's Mavis' house. If Howard was a part of the LLC, then Mavis should inherit that interest and be okay. If he wasn't, then Mavis..."

Conrad swallowed. "I was talking to Ned about these LLCs and he said an LLC passes through probate and is part of the deceased person's estate."

"Amanda couldn't find any record of a probate filed online. Doesn't mean it wasn't done, but I'm thinking maybe the LLC was not in Nora Bell's name when she died."

"That would mean Nora wouldn't have any assets so there wouldn't be a probate issue or inheritance tax to worry about," Conrad said. "A smart business person might have had Nora sign over that LLC before she passed away, just to avoid all that."

"That's the piece we can't seem to find," Cora said. "Maybe those LLC transfers aren't public record, or we aren't looking in the right place."

"I talked to Wanda today," Conrad said. "She thought the LLC was dissolved and said her parents never had much of anything, so Miriam took care of all the issues once her mom passed away."

"Oh, I bet she did." Cora took a bite of her sandwich and grabbed for another paper on the table. "This house is on Coriander Court."

Conrad took the deed showing Ned Carey sold it to the Stanton Bell, LLC. "Hmm," Conrad hummed as he chewed. "Who lives here?"

"Your fan, Karen Goldman," Cora said with a twisted smile. "The plot thickens."

"Okay," Conrad said wadding up his sandwich wrapper and brushing off his hands. "Let me see the list." .

"What list?"

"The list I know you've made of all this. You always make a list," Conrad said with his hand thrust out across the table.

Cora covered her mouth with one hand to keep from laughing with her mouth full and handed over her list of properties. She had residents listed for the three houses in town and estimates on the rural properties based on location.

Conrad looked through all the documents on the table waiting for Cora to finish her lunch. Picking up a pencil from the table, he added a name to the plat map. "The Nelson family was living out here last year," Conrad said tapping on the map. "They told me Miriam was their landlord and she was trying to evict them. I told them she had to file with the county to do it and I don't know if they still live there or not, but she must be managing the Stanton Bell, LLC properties."

"That's why no one can ever find her. She's

running around evicting people. I'm sure she loves that," Cora said tossing her head back as she picked up the lunch trash to clean off the table.

"Okay," Conrad said stretching back in his chair. "What are you thinking?"

"I think Miriam wants these seventeen properties and she tried to get Howard to sign over his interest in the LLC. I'm sure she offered to give him his own house and probably didn't even tell him what the LLC owned."

"Wanda told me Miriam had her sign something so she could handle the estate. I don't think she even knows what she signed, and Wanda believes there were no assets," Conrad said leaning forward. "I think Miriam got her mom to sign it over before she died telling her they could avoid taxes that way. Wanda thinks her mom's house was in a trust."

"Sounds like Wanda is the gullible child. We already know Miriam is the evil one and I've always heard Howard was a stubborn man. I bet he wouldn't give Miriam anything, especially after they stopped speaking to each other. That happened before Nora died."

"Yeah, Karen Goldman told me they had some falling out, but she was just a kid and didn't know why. She spoke fondly of her Uncle Howard."

"Have you ever asked Mavis?" Cora's eyebrows arched as she straightened her back.

"No, but I'm headed out there next and I will."

Sheri Richey

CHAPTER 24

"Hi, Amanda, Bryan," Conrad nodded to them both as they walked in. "I brought you a salad, Amanda. I didn't realize you'd left for lunch."

"Oh, thank you, Chief. I'll take it in the break room and put it in the frig for tomorrow."

"So, how is the flower business?" Conrad said to Bryan as Amanda left with her salad.

"Connie, it's not just flowers," Cora said rolling her eyes.

"Well, you get on to me if I say trees," Conrad said as Bryan laughed.

"It's going pretty well. I've still got a lot to do, but I'm getting some weekend business. Not much through the week though."

"Who mans the place when you come to town?" Conrad stood and pushed his chair in under the conference table.

"Leanne Summers is out there today so I was running a few errands," Bryan said as Amanda returned.

"I think I'm one of those errands," Amanda said smiling and kissing Bryan on the cheek, making him blush.

"I'm going to ride out with Connie to check on Mavis," Cora said to Amanda. "Have you seen Mavis at all, Bryan?"

"No, not once since they found out it was Howard. I don't think she's left the house. Leanne's husband, Jack, is in town though. I saw him this morning and Daniel has been by."

"Well, that's good that her family is close right now. I can't imagine what she must be going through having all this publicity and thinking all these years he might show up," Cora said shaking her head sadly.

"You ready?" Conrad said to Cora as she scurried to her desk to pull her purse from the drawer. Grabbing a small box of tissue, she stuffed it in her large satchel and hoisted the bag on her shoulder.

"Ready."

"Mandy, will you make me copies of all these deeds so I can pick them up when I come back?"

"Sure, Chief."

"Thank you. Let's go."

§

Conrad took his time driving through Spicetown to survey the activity on the main streets and process the information Cora had shared at lunch. Turning on the north road, he glanced over at Cora. "I need to talk to the kids too, if they're around. I don't know if they'll want to cooperate, but I need to know when they last saw Howard."

"I doubt you'll get as exact an answer as you did from Mavis. I don't think they miss Howard much."

"They were pretty young," Conrad said. "They probably just accepted Mavis' answer that he'd be back and weren't alarmed at the time."

"I hope she is honest about Miriam when you ask her," Cora said. "Mavis doesn't like to speak ill of anybody, but it's difficult to find anything glowing to say about Miriam Landry."

"Just because you don't like Miriam, doesn't mean she doesn't have friends," Conrad said chuckling as Cora scrunched up her nose.

"Name one," Cora barked.

Conrad laughed and shook his head. "Despite your speculation that Miriam had a motive, she didn't bury a body."

"True," Cora said with a pause. "I've thought about that and I can't think of anyone who would do anything like that for Miriam. Her husband was alive back then, but he wouldn't have been able to take on something that physically taxing. His health

227

was already bad, and he wasn't strong enough."

"I may have to walk over to Bryan's to talk to Leanne."

"I wonder if Jack and Leanne are getting along any better," Cora mused. "She seemed angry at him for visiting. I'm sure he's back now because of Howard."

"Has Daniel ever been married?"

"Not that I know of," Cora said. "He is one of those lost souls. He just never seemed to find his place in the world although he's tried a lot of different things. Mavis seems to think he is doing well at this job in Paxton now, but he still comes home every weekend. He's kind of a loner."

"Maybe he feels like he needs to take care of his mom." Conrad pulled in Mavis' driveway and saw Daniel in the yard squatted down beside a dirt bike. "Why don't you go in and check on Mavis and I'll talk to Daniel for a minute?"

"Okay," Cora said releasing her seatbelt and opening the car door. "Hi, Daniel." Cora waved as Daniel stood up.

"Hey there. Are you changing the oil?" Conrad approached Daniel as Cora walked up the steps to knock on the door.

"Yeah, it's been idle all winter," Daniel said as he wiped his hands on his jeans before accepting Conrad's extended hand.

"You've got a lot of room out here to run that bike. Conrad pointed out to the fields behind the house.

"Yeah, I thought I'd take the girls for a ride," Daniel said glancing over his shoulder. Leanne's daughters were in the backyard giggling on a trampoline. "If she'll let me." Daniel gave a smiling shrug.

"Daniel, I haven't had a chance to talk with you and I do have a couple of questions, if you don't mind."

"Sure," Daniel said sticking his hands in his jeans pockets.

"Do you remember the day Howard disappeared?"

"Kind of," Daniel said, shuffling his weight from one foot to the other.

"Can you tell me what you remember?"

"Just came home from school and he wasn't here. I didn't think much of it at the time."

"Was Leanne already here?"

"I don't think so. I think she came in right after."

"So, you weren't surprised or worried when you came home, and he wasn't here."

"No," Daniel said looking at the ground as he scuffed his toe in the dirt. "Sometimes he had things to do."

"So, when did you think something was amiss? Dinner time?"

"Yeah, I guess. I don't remember."

"So, did the house seem normal when you arrived that day? Anything out of place? Was there a car in the drive?"

"Mom had the car. She was at work."

"How did you get home from school?"

"I took the bus. Jack brought Leanne home."

"So how did Howard leave during the day if he had to run errands?"

"He had a motorcycle." Daniel pointed to the small shed on the back of the property.

"It was December," Conrad said. "He rode it in the winter?"

"Yeah, if he needed to," Daniel said looking at his feet again.

"So, what did you think happened when Howard didn't come home?"

"I just figured they got in a fight and he'd be back," Daniel shrugged. "I didn't think it was anything serious."

"And when he didn't return?"

"I just figured he'd moved on. People split sometimes." Another shrug and more swaying were all he offered Conrad.

"Did you and Howard get along?" Conrad ducked his head down under Daniel's lowered head to get Daniel to look him in the eye.

"Sometimes."

Conrad sighed heavily to rein in his frustration. "Look, I know parents and teenagers bicker. It's normal, but overall—"

"Howard wasn't my dad."

"I know. He was your stepdad, but you'd lived with him for a long time."

"Yeah, we argued some. Howard could be a real jerk sometimes, but he was okay."

Conrad gave up. Hopefully, his sister would be more forthcoming. "I'm going to go in and check on your mom, now. Do you guys need anything? Is she doing all right?"

"Yeah, she's worried about a funeral and stuff."

"Has Miriam been out here again?"

"Yeah, she was here this morning."

Conrad raised his eyebrows and nodded his head trying to encourage Daniel to continue but he did not take the hint. "And? Was she helpful?"

"I don't know. I was outside but Miriam looked mad when she left."

Conrad nodded and turned toward the front steps of the house.

"Come in. Hi, Chief," Mavis said when Conrad tapped on the door as he opened it.

"Hey, Mavis. Just checking in on you. How are things going?"

"Mavis was just telling me Miriam visited again today," Cora said before Mavis could respond.

"Yes, Daniel told me. Was it any better than last time?"

"Maybe a little," Mavis said smiling shyly. "Or maybe I handled it better this time."

"What exactly does Miriam want? Is it about the funeral? Or is it about the house?" Conrad took a seat in the living room where the ladies were sitting.

"A little of both," Mavis said sighing.

"So, where do you stand legally with the house? Did Howard inherit part of the LLC when his mother died?"

"Cora and I were just discussing that. From what I know," Mavis said sitting back on the sofa, "Howard and his sisters own the company now and the company owns the house. I think the property was owned by Howard's great-great-grandfather or something."

"So now, you and the sisters own the company?" Cora said seeking clarification.

"I think it's just me and Miriam." Mavis shrugged and looked down at her hands. "Howard told me Miriam stole it from Wanda and she wasn't taking it from him. They fought about it after his mom died."

"So, when Nora died, Howard found out his sister, Wanda, lost her share?"

"It wasn't then," Mavis corrected. "Howard just found this out right before he disappeared. They had been arguing about it and he told me Miriam was trying to rob us blind." Mavis huffed. "Pfft, I just laughed at him. I didn't think we had anything worth takin'. I just thought it was them bickerin' again. Miriam is a hard woman to get along with."

"So, you didn't know about the LLC?" Conrad asked.

"Oh, I knew it owned our house and I knew it was his family land. I didn't know any particulars until this all blew up with Miriam."

"What caused the blow up?" Cora asked.

"Miriam said Howard asked her to cosign a loan against the house. I know that's not the case, but she doesn't think I know any better."

"So, what did happen?" Cora said.

"Howard went to the bank and tried to get a mortgage on the house. With him out of work and me just starting at the drugstore, things were tight. The bank told him the mortgage would have to be done with the LLC because they owned the house, so he had to talk to his sisters. They would have to agree."

"That's how Howard found out Wanda had signed over her part?" Conrad said nodding.

"Yes, and Miriam offered to sign over the house to him if he signed over the LLC," Mavis said clasping her hands in her lap.

"Howard didn't go for that?" Conrad imagined a power struggle ensued and Miriam didn't like to lose.

"No," Mavis said shaking her head. "He said Miriam was trying to rip him off and he should be drawing a check every month from the rent money she collected. He said the LLC owned a lot of things that made money."

"So, he had never received any compensation from it? Even after his mother died?" Cora's face twisted up as if she were tasting something bitter.

"No, I didn't know we should be, but Howard said he was going to make her turn over the books. He saw some lawyer over in Paxton about it."

"I thought Howard and Miriam weren't even speaking," Cora said.

"They hadn't in a long time," Mavis said. "It was hard for him to go talk to her about the mortgage because they hadn't spoken in years. After that, she was out here yelling at him, just like she did me the other day. Difference was, Howard would throw her right out." Mavis chuckled in the pleasurable memory. "Didn't stop her though. She just kept at him. He never went to see her again as far as I know."

"How far did the legal process get?" Cora asked.

"I know they served her with papers, but Howard disappeared before it was dealt with."

"When was the last time Miriam visited Howard?" Conrad said as he pulled a small notebook out of his pocket.

"Most of the time she came during the day when I was at work. He'd tell me about it that night. I think she was here the last day Howard was because when I came home that night, Miriam's leather gloves were on my kitchen table. At least I think they were hers."

"Do you still have them?" Cora asked moving to the edge of her seat.

"I do," Mavis said jumping up from the sofa and going to the coat closet near the front door. "I wear them in the winter myself," she said smiling. "She's never asked for them back and if they belonged to some other woman, I figured she owed me as much if she took my Howard away. I guess I kind of wore them out of spite." Mavis smiled and handed the black leather gloves to Conrad. "They're real nice. They got that soft fur inside and fit real good."

"You know, Mavis," Conrad said earnestly, "You really might want to contact that lawyer yourself. I think Miriam might owe you a whole lot of money and you need to know where you stand. It sounds like you are in business with Miriam now and that might be something you need to take care of."

"It's not worth getting killed over, Chief. I don't want to go to war with Miriam."

"Do you think she might have killed Howard?" Cora asked in disbelief.

"No, I didn't mean it like that. Howard never had any trouble throwing her out the door. I don't think she meant him any harm like that. She just can't stand it when people don't do what she wants."

Conrad looked at the gloves in his hand and wished Mavis hadn't worn them. It would be nearly impossible to link them to Miriam now after all these years.

"Mavis, if you don't deal with the LLC now, your kids could be stuck dealing with Miriam later," Cora said holding her hands up in a defensive motion. "We never know what the future holds and leaving things the way they are…"

"Yeah," Mavis said thoughtfully. "You're probably right. I hadn't thought about that. It'd be easier to just take her deal and then at least the kids would have this house in peace."

"No, I didn't mean that," Cora said. "You should get what is due to you and to Howard. I know he would want you to do that. You should follow through on what Howard started. You don't want to let Miriam win just because she behaves badly."

"I know you wouldn't, Cora," Mavis said shrugging. "You're a fighter for things you believe in, but I just don't have that in me. I just want a peaceful life."

"Look, I know she's difficult, but she can be stopped. I'll help you file for an order to keep her off the property. She can't come over here and—"

"No," Mavis said with a dismissive wave. "Cora, I don't want all that. I just want to keep her at arm's length until I get through the funeral. Then I'll settle up with her." Mavis nodded her head decidedly. "It'll be fine."

"Well, just know we are here to help you," Conrad said. "Have you made funeral arrangements?"

"Still working on those details with the coroner's office, but yes, it's coming along. He has a plot already with his family and I'm going to bury him next to his daddy."

"That's nice," Cora said. "We will certainly be at the service."

"Thank you."

"Mavis, are the kids going to stay with you until the funeral?" Conrad stood up and hiked his pants up.

"Yes, Leanne is over at the nursery now and Jack is here, too."

"I'm sure that's a comfort," Cora said standing to walk to the door with Conrad.

"It is," Mavis said hugging Cora and squeezing Conrad's hand before opening the door for them.

"You call me if you need anything," Cora said through the screen door and Mavis nodded.

Daniel and the motorcycle were gone.

Sheri Richey

CHAPTER 25

"Do you want me to take you back and then I'll come talk to Leanne?" Conrad said as they returned to his car.

"Oh, no. I'll ride along. I can look around while you talk. There's no need for you to come back out here." Cora waved again at Mavis who was standing at the door, but once the car doors were both shut, she pivoted in her seat toward Conrad.

"Can you *believe* that woman? Howard was right. She was robbing them both blind and they are her own flesh and blood. Poor Wanda was sick, and Howard worked hard his whole life and she couldn't give either of them even a crumb. The woman is a thief and a liar. How can she live with herself? Something has to be done. Conrad, you have to do something. What she's done is criminal. It's theft!"

"Cora, I don't disagree, but those charges have to be brought by the injured parties. You need to pull it all back in because we're already here," Conrad said as he pulled in the parking lot of the nursery.

Cora huffed loudly and turned back in her seat. "Can't very well file charges with your own cousin, can you?"

"Hmm," Conrad paused to consider the fact Mavis was in Bobby's Bell's jurisdiction. "It might be awkward." Conrad released his seatbelt and opened the door. "Maybe you'd like to wait in the car?"

Not waiting for a response from Cora, Conrad waved to Leanne who was out under the canopy beside the greenhouse.

"Hey, Chief. Can I help you find something?"

"No, I was just passing by and thought I'd stop and talk to you for a minute. I was just up at the house checking on your mom and she said you were down here."

"Yeah, Bryan had some errands to run so I'm keeping an eye on the place until he gets back."

"I saw Daniel at the house earlier and talked to him a bit, but I'd like to get your take on a few things, too."

"I saw Daniel ride by. He's working on that old motorbike. He thinks he's taking my kids out on it, but he better think again," Leanne said laughing.

"Well, they can be dangerous," Conrad said nodding. "I was asking Daniel about the day

Howard disappeared. Do you remember that day?"

"Yeah, a little. It wasn't really a special day, I mean we didn't think it was going to be. We thought he'd be back," Leanne said apologetically.

"So, you came home from school that day?"

"Yeah, Jack had a car and he always drove me home. We'd stopped at the gas station after school, so Daniel got home first. We weren't worried though. Sometimes Howard wasn't there."

"When did you realize something wasn't right?" Conrad asked.

"When mom got home, I asked her because he was usually home by that time. She acted like she didn't want to talk about it, so I thought they'd had a fight or something. I didn't ask again. I mean, it wasn't my business, really."

"Were you ever home or around when Miriam visited Howard?"

"Yeah, I saw her a few times, but I stayed clear of that. I always found some reason to leave if she showed up. She wasn't very nice to me or to Daniel."

"So, you never heard what they talked about?"

"Oh, I heard yelling. I mean Howard would just throw her out, tell her to leave. The talks didn't last long."

"Do you know what they were fighting about?"

"Miriam had done something," Leanne said shrugging. "He kept saying things like 'I can't believe you'd do that to your own family'. Things like that. I don't know what she did."

"Did you get along well with Howard?"

"Yeah, I mean we argued some, but he was okay. He didn't like me spending so much time with Jack, so we fought about that sometimes. It wasn't that he didn't like Jack or anything. He just was afraid we were together too much, you know. He didn't want me to get in trouble."

"I understand," Conrad said. "Where is Jack? Mavis said he was home, too."

"Oh, he's running around town somewhere. Wanted to see some people while he was here. He still keeps in touch with some friends we went to school with." Leanne cocked her head to the side and held up her finger. "Do you hear that?"

Conrad listened and heard the faint sound of a motor running.

"That's Daniel. He must be driving that bike in the fields up there," Leanne said pointing to the Christmas tree farm. "We did that as kids all the time, but there weren't trees up there then."

"Oh, you had a bike, too?"

"No, but the old bike he used had a really neat sidecar on it. Howard got it at some flea market and fixed it up so I could ride in it. I never drove the bikes, but it was fun riding along. Daniel thinks we need another one of those so the girls can ride. I don't know if I want that to happen though." Leanne chuckled and sighed. "It's different when it's your kids."

"I'm sure it is," Conrad said smiling. He thanked her and returned to his car where Cora sat still brooding.

Cora waved at Leanne as Conrad slid into the driver's seat. "She said Jack's in town somewhere visiting friends."

"Was she helpful?"

"Yes," Conrad said brooding over his thoughts. "A whole lot easier to talk to than Daniel was."

"Leanne's an actress," Cora said.

"What do you mean?"

"I mean she can turn it on and off," Cora said. "One minute she can seem angry and the next, she can smile sweetly. She can turn on tears like a switch. I remember her as a child, and you could never tell what the real girl inside was feeling. Now Daniel, he can't express himself. He can't figure out how to convey how he feels when Leanne can fake any feeling at all. They're an odd couple of kids."

"Hm, interesting," Conrad said. "Did you know their dad?"

"I knew of him, but Clarence died before I had either of the kids in my class. They were really young. I think Mavis and Clarence were high school sweethearts though. They married young."

"Mavis has had some rough luck," Conrad said.

"Can you do anything with those old gloves?"

"Nah, I don't think so," Conrad said shaking his head. "I'll turn them in, but I'm sure any traces of the owner are gone with Mavis wearing them over the years.

"Yeah, I figured as much."

"What do you know about Jack Summers?" Conrad asked as he turned and slowed down to enter the city limits.

"He was a good kid," Cora said. "Studious as I recall. He has a head on his shoulders. I always thought he'd go to college and have a career. I never thought he'd get married right out of high school."

"Was Leanne pregnant?"

"No, not that I ever heard. I know the two girls were born much later, but it's always possible she was and lost the baby. I always thought Jack married her because she told him to. I'm sure you've noticed he's pretty passive and Leanne is bossy."

"But I thought you were concerned when he showed up that first day at the nursery. I thought you were worried about Leanne."

"Oh, heaven's no," Cora said smiling. "I was afraid Leanne would make a scene. She's famous for public displays of anger. I was under the impression they were having problems, possibly separating, so when he showed up, I thought he was going to grovel, and Leanne was going to act out."

"Oh, I misunderstood your concerns that day."

"Are you going to interview Jack?"

"If I can find him. Leanne and Daniel both say he was there that day. He brought her home from school."

"I'm sure he got along with Howard well, but he

was probably intimidated by him somewhat. Jack will be afraid to talk to you though. He'll be afraid Leanne doesn't want him to.

"Did you ask either of the kids about Miriam? Do they get along with her?"

"Leanne said Miriam wasn't very nice to either of them."

"Did you tell her she was a member of a very large club?" Cora said laughing.

§

After dropping Cora off at City Hall with plans to meet for dinner, Conrad went in the side door of the police department. Dropping the gloves Mavis had given him on his desk, he picked up his pitcher to go fill it with water and make some coffee. He needed to read through the material Amanda had copied for him and make some notes on his interviews. While filling the pitcher with water in the break room, Georgia Marks tracked him down.

"Chief, Miriam Landry is out there. She's in the waiting room and wants to talk to you."

"Okay," Conrad groaned. "Give me a minute to get my coffee started and I'll come get her."

"She's been waiting not so patiently for about ten minutes, but she'll tell you she's been there an hour."

"I'm sure I'll hear about it," Conrad chuckled and carried his water back to his office.

With the water poured in, he turned the coffee maker on and turned around as Miriam came through his office door.

"You were just going to leave me sitting out there all day?" Miriam said with her hand on her hip.

"I was starting some coffee. I thought you might want some," Conrad said motioning Miriam to a chair. "Have a seat, Miriam. How can I help you?"

"I know you are out there in town spreading rumors about me and I want it to stop. I want you to stay away from my family," Miriam said ignoring the chair as Conrad walked around and sat at his desk.

"I don't know what you are referring to, Miriam. I'm certainly not spreading any rumors."

"Howard is dead. My brother is dead. What are you doing about that? You're running around asking questions about me. Me!" Miriam yelled. "You haven't even talked to Carmen Maddox."

Conrad couldn't stop his eyebrows from raising. "You have reason to believe Carmen Maddox is involved in your brother's death?"

"Of course, I do!" Miriam screeched. "Everyone does."

"You're the first person to tell me that," Conrad said calmly. "Please, sit down. Tell me why you feel that way."

"What are you doing with my gloves?" Miriam

began to snatch them from Conrad's desk, but he grabbed them first. "Where did you get them?"

"Where did you leave them?" Conrad said smiling.

Miriam huffed with indignation. "Leave me alone, Conrad, and leave my family alone."

"I thought you wanted me to find out who killed your brother," Conrad said, raising his voice as she stormed out of his office.

Conrad leaned back in his chair and allowed himself a good laugh. Maybe he should take Miriam up on her advice.

Sheri Richey

CHAPTER 26

"Mayor," Amanda said as her head popped around the edge of the door. "Rodney is here to see you."

"Oh, Rodney," Cora called out waving him in the door. "Come on in."

"Afternoon, Mayor," Rodney said lowering his head. "I'm sorry to bother you. I just wanted to catch you before you left today and give you the pictures." Rodney handed Cora a large sturdy folder and she spread it out over her desk.

"Oh, Rodney. These are fantastic. Amanda, come see."

Amanda walked around the desk and peered over Cora's shoulder. "Wow, those are great, Rodney. They'll work really well when we reprint them, I think."

"Yes," Cora agreed. "I think they're just perfect. And this one," Cora said pointing. "The train track and station behind him is just the best touch. I love them."

"Thank you," Rodney said shyly. "I was hoping you'd like them."

"Rodney," Cora said looking up. "You really have a talent. You really do."

Rodney shrugged it off and colored with embarrassment. "It's just copying."

"It's brilliant," Cora said. "Amanda, can you go make Rodney a check?"

"Sure."

"Have a seat, Rodney. It'll just take a minute. I'm very pleased with the picture. Do you enjoy doing this type of thing?"

"Oh, yeah. It's kind of a hobby. I've always liked to draw and try to copy things. Carmen calls them doodles," he said smiling.

"How is Carmen? Are things going better now?"

"She's good. She was upset about Howard Bell. She said he was a very nice man. It's a horrible thing," Rodney said hanging his head lower.

"Did you know him?" Cora asked.

"No. I knew the name, but I don't think we ever met. Carmen knew him because she worked out in the mine payroll office years ago. She wasn't there very long, but Howard was a foreman out there and he came in the office some. She said he was always nice to her."

"Well, you know, Rodney, there were all those

rumors…"

"Yeah, I know about all that, but it's not true. Carmen said someone spread all those rumors because they were mad at Andrew. They were trying to shame Andrew, but it was really Carmen that was hurt by it."

"Has Carmen ever tried to talk to the person about this?"

"Oh, yeah, back when it was all going on. I don't guess she got anywhere with it though. That all happened before we started seeing each other but, I admit, I heard those rumors too."

"Yes, it was prevalent," Cora agreed. "It's very unfair when someone slanders you and you can't stop them."

"She was already going through so much back then with her marriage having trouble and being pregnant. I don't know how she got through it all."

"I hate it that this has dredged all this up for her, but soon maybe it will all be over for good."

"I don't know," Rodney said shaking his head. "People do love to gossip."

"Human nature," Cora said as Amanda returned with Rodney's check. "Well, thank you for this and I'll contact you again if we need your services."

"Yes, ma'am. I'm happy to help anytime. Thank you."

§

"Mrs. Maddox? This is Chief Harris of the Spicetown Police Department. Do you have a minute to speak with me?"

"Sure, Chief," Carmen said, sighing. "I expected to hear from you, eventually."

"Well, I'm told you knew Howard Bell, so I'm just reaching out to everybody I can. I didn't have the pleasure of meeting the man."

"Howard was a very nice guy. We worked together a short time and he was always pleasant."

"Did you have a personal relationship with Howard Bell?"

"No," Carmen said adamantly. "Those are all empty rumors that his sister, Miriam, spread around town."

"Why would his sister do that?"

"She was mad at my husband, my first husband, Andrew Gentry. Andrew had a business here in town, but he wouldn't join the Chamber of Commerce. He and Miriam didn't get along. I don't know all the details, but she started bad-mouthing him and making up stories trying to hurt his business. It wasn't just these things about Howard. She told other stories about Andrew to try to discourage people from doing business with him. They were just feuding, and I got caught in the middle."

"What kind of business did your husband have?" Conrad asked.

"He had a tire store and they did oil and belt changes. Not a full mechanic shop, but more like an auto maintenance type of place over on Sumac Street, just off Paprika Parkway."

"When was the last time you recall seeing Howard Bell?"

"I saw him in the Sweet & Sour Spice Shop about two months or so before I heard he was missing. It was in the fall that year and we were both shopping. He said hello and asked about my son. We chatted for a few minutes while he was paying for something he bought for his wife. It was a perfectly normal thing. There was nothing more between us than being acquaintances. He's probably twenty years older than me. The rumors are crazy."

"Well, I appreciate your time," Conrad said. "I'm sorry I had to bother you with this."

"It's fine, Chief. I understand. You're welcome to talk to my ex-husband if you like. He doesn't live here anymore but I can give you his number. He might be able to explain more about why the rumors started."

"That won't be necessary," Conrad said. "I've already spoken to him today and he said much the same. I'm just covering all of my bases."

"Okay," Carmen said. "I understand."

"Thank you, Mrs. Maddox. You have a good day now."

"Thank you, Chief. You, too."

§

Conrad waved at Joanne Biglioni as he slid in the booth across from Cora at the Ole Thyme Italian Restaurant.

"Connie, I'm about to admit something here, so brace yourself."

Conrad smiled, never knowing what to expect next from Cora. "Okay, I'm ready."

"I may have been wrong about Carmen Maddox." Cora slid her eyes sideways to glance sheepishly at Conrad.

"Hmm."

"Not about everything, mind you, but maybe about this Howard Bell connection. Maybe she was the victim in all that gossip and I actually, just for a minute today, I actually felt sorry for her."

"I agree with you," Conrad said. "Miriam paid me a visit today and pretty much confirmed that."

"Really?" Cora said sitting back in shock. "Miriam told you Carmen wasn't involved with Howard?"

"No, she actually told me I should be investigating Carmen," Conrad said cocking his head to the side. "So, I called Carmen."

"Really? Wow, you have had a busy afternoon. What did Carmen say?"

"Well, brace yourself. I'm about to admit something here," Conrad said as Cora giggled. "She was actually quite nice and seemed perfectly normal when I had painted her a lunatic years ago. She told me Miriam was mad at Andrew because he wouldn't join the Chamber and she spread all kinds of hateful things about him around town. She used his wife in part of those stories, and it was just juicy enough to catch on, I guess."

"Good grief," Cora said taking a deep breath. "What a mess. I guess what Rodney told me was true. Carmen got caught in the middle and was a victim."

"I think so, yeah," Conrad said.

"Such a shame," Cora said as Jo approached the table to take their order.

Once their drinks arrived and their orders were placed, Conrad turned back to Cora. "It was actually a good thing Miriam came in today."

"Oh, she was pleasant this time?"

"No, but she was helpful while in a fit of rage. I don't think she likes me much," Conrad said as Cora laughed.

"Like I said earlier today, it's a big club. How was her rage helpful?"

"She identified her gloves for me," Conrad winked and smiled. "That's what happens when your anger gets the best of you. You speak without thinking first."

"Oh, I can personally vouch for that," Cora admitted.

§

"Listen," Amanda whispered. "It sounds like

somebody is out there."

Bryan frowned but heard nothing. "Maybe it's the wind. Do you want some more tea?"

"No, thank you," Amanda said smiling as Bryan started clearing the table. "Dinner was very good."

"I'm glad you liked it," Bryan said freezing in his stance between the chair and the kitchen sink with plates in both hands. "I think I heard something."

"I didn't hear a car drive in," Amanda said as she went to the front window and peered out. "No, there's nobody here."

"I'm going to go out there and look around," Bryan said placing the dirty dishes beside the sink.

"No, don't do that," Amanda said. "What if it's a wild animal? Just wait."

"If it's an animal, it'll take off when I go out there. I don't want anything getting into the greenhouse."

"I'll go with you," Amanda said protectively, reaching to slide her phone in her back pocket.

"No, you stay here. I'll just be a minute."

Amanda followed him to the kitchen door with every intention of ignoring his instruction, just as they both gasped at the sound of the bell ringing in the garden.

CHAPTER 27

"That's not an animal," Amanda whispered. "You need to call the sheriff's office."

"If someone's trying to steal something, they don't ring a bell to say they're out there," Bryan said reaching for the doorknob.

"Wait. We need a weapon," Amanda said looking around the room. She grabbed a garden trowel and Bryan reached on the shelf for a flashlight before opening the door.

"Stay here," Bryan whispered again but didn't protest when he felt Amanda closely following. Flipping on the outside lights they walked across the front of the house and looked towards the greenhouse. Bryan pointed his flashlight at the bell in the garden and saw a figure stumbling to stand.

"Oh, guys, sorry, oh." The man pulled himself up leaning on the bell stand and turned around squinting from the flashlight beam trained on him.

"Jack?" Bryan said in surprise. "What are you doing out here?"

"Oh my," Amanda said with her hand on her chest. "You scared me to death, Jack."

"So sorry. I didn't mean to. I was walking around, walking over in the dark. I forgot about the bell and…"

"Come inside," Bryan said reaching out to pat Jack on the back. "We're just finishing dinner. Come in and have a drink with us."

Jack nodded as he shuffled along beside Bryan and Amanda followed with a scrutinizing frown.

"How about some coffee?" Amanda suggested and darted her eyes at Bryan trying to convey her concerns Jack might be intoxicated.

"So, what brings you out on a walk tonight?" Bryan picked up the remaining dishes from the table and moved them to the counter as Jack sat down.

"It's pretty heavy over there," Jack said motioning to Mavis' house next door. "I needed to take a walk and clear my head for a few minutes. I thought you might be out in the greenhouse. I didn't mean to interrupt."

"It's no interruption," Amanda said as she rinsed the dinner dishes at the sink. "We were just finishing up."

"Has Mavis made all the arrangements now?" Bryan asked.

"I guess. It's just with everybody there, you

know. I couldn't think. This whole thing is really messed up and I've tried to talk to them, but they won't listen to me."

"It's really tragic," Bryan said taking the mug Amanda handed him and sitting it in front of Jack.

"I told them they need to tell the truth and just get it out straight so maybe there's a chance to make it all right."

Amanda frowned at Bryan with concern. "You mean Mavis?" Amanda said cautiously.

"No, Daniel and Leanne," Jack said blowing on his coffee. "I mean, they don't know who killed Howard or anything, but they know how he got out there," Jack said waving his hand towards the Christmas tree farm. "Maybe it would help the police find out what really happened to Howard."

"Maybe you need to tell the Chief yourself," Amanda said sitting down at the table. "I could call him and I'm sure he'd come out here."

"Leanne would kill me," Jack said and then sputtered with laughter. "I don't mean that literally, of course, but I'd be in some big trouble with her."

"Are you and Leanne having problems?" Bryan asked cautiously. "I mean it looked like you were arguing when you talked to her here at the nursery."

"Oh, that's just normal stuff," Jack said with a sneer.

"Is she wanting to move back home?" Amanda asked. "You're still working in St. Louis, aren't you?"

"Yeah, she wants to move back. I don't think I can find work here though. We've argued about that a thousand times."

"So, why is it that Daniel and Leanne are keeping secrets from the police? Do they think they know who killed Howard?"

"No, I don't think so," Jack said slurping his hot coffee. "They're just afraid they'll get in trouble or that Mavis would get upset. I think it's time they do the right thing."

"But maybe *you* need to do the right thing. I mean, you've got to live with this knowledge too, and you have to do what you think is best. If they aren't going to do it, maybe you need to talk to the Chief." Amanda pulled her phone out of her pocket and put it on the table. "We can do that right now."

"Yeah, Jack," Bryan nodded. "I'm sure it would be a big relief to get that off your chest and see if it makes a difference. You could be what solves this whole case."

"You're probably right," Jack said sitting his coffee cup down firmly. "I might lose my wife and kids over it though. I don't know if I'm willing to do that."

"If they didn't kill him, I don't see how they would get in trouble," Bryan said shrugging. "It might just give them clues they need to find who did."

"My argument exactly," Jack said tapping his fist on the table. "They aren't convinced though."

"I understand if you do this, you might not be able to mend that fence with Leanne, but you won't lose your kids," Amanda said. "I mean, you'll always be their father and you'll always be able to see them. The way it looks right now, Leanne isn't going back to St. Louis anyway and she put the kids in school here."

"Did she say anything to you?" Jack asked with alarm.

"Only that she wanted to stay, and she thought the kids were doing well here in the school and seeing Mavis regularly. She sounded like she was happy to stay here. Unless you plan to move, it sounds like you may be living apart, anyway. I mean I thought you two were separating."

"We've talked about it," Jack said sadly. "Mostly over the move. The problem is that if I don't just do whatever she wants, my life is miserable. I love her, but what she wants isn't always the right thing to do."

"I understand," Bryan said nodding. "But sometimes you have to do the right thing so you can live with yourself. It sounds like this secret might be something that has haunted you a long time and that can wear on a relationship too."

"Let me see if the Chief is free and let's just take care of this now. You can't go on like this forever," Amanda implored.

"You're right," Jack said nodding. "I've gone back and forth a million times and it's never going to be over. I'm ready for it to be over."

Amanda got up from the table and slipped her phone in her hand. "I'll just give him a call."

§

"Mayor," Amanda said in a low voice from the living room. "I need you to call the Chief and see if he can come out to Bryan's right now please. I don't have his number."

"The Chief is right here, honey," Cora said giving Conrad a concerned glance. "What's wrong?"

"Jack Summers is out here, and he knows something about Howard Bell. He's ready to talk right now and I don't want him to change his mind."

"We're on our way," Cora said grabbing at her purse handles and motioning frantically to Conrad to get to the car. "Does he know who killed him?" Cora whispered as they walked out the door of the Ole Thyme Italian Restaurant. Conrad pulled the door open for Cora and ran around the car to jump in.

"No, but he knows something about how he got in Bryan's garden. I think he's been drinking, but he doesn't seem drunk."

"We're pulling out now," Cora said as she struggled with the seatbelt clip while holding the phone. "Jack Summers is at Bryan's house. He wants to talk," Cora said to Conrad.

"Is he alone?" Conrad asked.

"Is he there alone?" Cora asked Amanda.

"Yes, he walked over here," Amanda said as Cora nodded to Conrad. "He's pretty troubled by the knowledge he has and is afraid of angering Leanne, so he keeps waffling. I hope he is still willing to talk to you when you get here."

"We're moving as fast as we can. Keep him talking and give him coffee."

"Okay, I'll see you soon. Thanks," Amanda said going back in the kitchen.

"He'll be here shortly," Amanda said nonchalantly as she walked to the sink. "Maybe I should make some more coffee?"

"I sure hope I don't regret this," Jack said rubbing his hand over his face.

"I think you'll be relieved," Amanda said. "All of this anxiety and worry will be over, and it might even really help Mavis out if she doesn't know the truth."

"No, she doesn't know. They didn't want her involved."

"People need closure," Bryan said. "I think it will really help resolve part of the mystery for Mavis and help her out. She's been through a lot. This was a big shock for her."

"Yeah, Mavis is good people," Jack nodded in agreement as he took a drink of his coffee.

"I know death is hard to deal with when it is someone close. Even when you are prepared or you think you are prepared, it still shakes your world."

"Your folks were really great people, too," Jack said smiling. "Your dad was always trying to teach me something and your mom would try to feed me. I loved coming over here and seeing them."

"Yeah, I miss them, and I still think about them. Even though I knew I was going to lose them, I still had a hard time accepting it when it happened," Bryan said regretfully.

"Poor Mavis has had to go through that loss twice now. She thought she lost Howard back when he disappeared and now, she learns he's really gone. I can't imagine how she must feel," Amanda said as she refilled Jack's coffee cup.

"That bell," Jack said chuckling. "I can't believe I forgot it was there and walked right into it. Howard used to send me over here sometimes to ring it for Daniel. I guess he had some arrangement with your dad."

"Yeah, Dad used to get after me when I was a kid because I'd ring it and he'd come back to the house. He thought mom wanted him and it was just me playing around. He'd tell me I shouldn't ring the bell unless I meant it."

"I'm sure he was afraid to ignore it in case your mom really needed something," Amanda said as she heard gravel crunching in the lot from a car pulling up.

"Yeah, I was just fooling around, and he was right. Kids are just drawn to it though." Bryan got up from the table as he saw the Chief and the mayor walking toward the door.

"I heard it ring several times on opening day," Amanda said smiling at Jack. "There were a lot of kids out here and they just can't resist it."

CHAPTER 28

"Hi, Jack," Conrad said extending his hand to shake. "I guess you know the mayor."

"Oh, yes," Cora said smiling. "We go way back."

"Hi, Chief," Jack said standing and accepting Conrad's hand. "Mayor."

"Can I make you some tea?" Amanda asked Cora.

"No, thank you, dear. I just had some."

"Coffee, Chief?"

"Yeah, I'll take some," Conrad said pulling out a kitchen chair to sit down.

Cora wandered into the living room and Bryan casually followed her.

"Here you go. There's more over there," Amanda said pointing to the counter. "I'll leave you alone and let you talk. Just holler if you need anything."

"Thank you," Conrad said turning to Jack. "I was planning to talk with you. I was out at Mavis' earlier today and came by here, too. They told me you were in town."

"I thought about coming by the station earlier, but I just wasn't sure…"

"I understand," Conrad said, "but I'm sure you know what the right thing here is, son. Mavis needs to know the truth and if what you know might help us find out, you need to share what you know."

"Yeah," Jack said nodding. "I don't think I can keep going with it any longer.

"So, you know who buried Howard out back?"

Jack rubbed his hand over his face. "Yeah, it was us. We came home from school and found him dead."

"Who exactly do you mean by us? You and Leanne?"

"And Daniel. I mean I guess it was mainly me and Daniel," Jack said shrugging.

"Help me understand," Conrad said gently. "Why did you feel his body needed to be hidden? Why didn't you just call police?"

"That's what I wanted to do," Jack said emphatically. "I even picked up the phone and started to call, but Leanne took the phone away and said we couldn't do that."

"Why do you think she felt that way?"

"I thought at first she was protecting Mavis. I couldn't believe Mavis would kill anybody, but maybe they got in a fight and it was an accident or something. I thought Leanne was protecting her mom."

"You don't think that now?" Conrad said taking a sip of his coffee.

"No, I mean she's never really told me, but it just seems crazy to think it was Mavis. Then I thought maybe she thought it was Daniel. He got home before we did, but later I knew that wasn't it either."

"Later?"

"Well, I mean I was a stupid kid when all this happened. I didn't understand Rigor Mortis and stuff like that. Now I know Howard didn't just die right before I got there."

"Oh, I see," Conrad said nodding. "His body was cold?"

"Yeah, and parts were getting, you know, stiff."

"So, how was Daniel through all this? I mean, Leanne tells you to hang up and not call the police. What did Daniel say? Did he have any suggestion or…?"

"No, he was pretty freaked out when we walked in. I think he had just gotten there, and he didn't know what to do."

"So, Leanne makes the decisions for both of

you. She tells you two to bury him?"

"Yeah, that's pretty much it. Bryan didn't live here back then. We knew it was a vacant house. I mean people had lived here off and on, but at the time we knew it was empty." Jack tipped up his coffee and sat it down when he realized it was empty.

"Did you use the motorcycle?" Conrad asked as he got up from the table and got the coffee pot.

"Yeah," Jack said raising his head up.

"Put him in the side car?"

"Yeah. How did you know?" Jack said incredulously. "You already knew that?"

"I thought it was a real possibility," Conrad said as he refilled Jack's cup and returned the coffee pot.

"Oh, wow, okay," Jack said sighing with relief. "I don't have any idea why he died though or if someone did something to him. He wasn't bleeding or anything. I mean maybe he just died alone."

"Tell me about the house," Conrad said sitting back down at the table. "What did it look like when you walked in? Where was Howard?"

"Oh, well, when we pulled up Daniel was on the porch pacing. He was really upset and making no sense at all. We ran in the house and Howard was on his back in the middle of the living room floor staring at the ceiling."

"Daniel knew he was dead?"

"Yeah, I didn't ask how, but he told us that

when, well, first thing."

"Maybe Leanne thought Daniel killed him."

"Maybe," Jack said. "But he was in school all day just like us. I mean he rode the bus home and I saw him during the day. I knew he was at school."

"Like you said though, now you know that he hadn't just died, but back then you didn't know about Rigor Mortis."

"Yeah, I might have thought that back then. Leanne might have, too. I don't think that now."

"So now that you know better, you thought they ought to tell Mavis," Conrad said.

"Right," Jack said. "I mean none of us thought she did it and we didn't do it, so it's time to try to find out who did. I'm guessing they think they'll get in trouble. Can you get in trouble for just burying somebody?"

"Disturbing a body and not reporting a crime is a fourth-degree misdemeanor," Conrad admitted. "But concealing evidence that could further an investigation is a lot more serious. You were right to tell us. I'm sorry they wouldn't listen to you."

"I don't want anybody to get in trouble. I just need to know I did what I could to help find out the truth."

"Was the house disturbed at all? Anything knocked over? Anything out of place?"

"Not that I remember," Jack said staring off blankly at a spot on the wall. "It was, you know, we were upset. It's all kind of fuzzy, but I don't remember anything different."

"Was there snow on the ground that day?"

"No," Jack said. "It was cool outside but not even as cold as usual for December. I remember thinking we wouldn't be able to dig. You know, the ground would be hard, but it wasn't."

"So, nothing in the house that didn't belong?"

"Ah," Jack said running his hands through his hair. "I wish I could remember. All I could focus on was Howard and what we were going to do. I don't think I even looked but there was nothing obvious. Surely, I would have noticed if there was something really different. I wish I could be more help."

"Don't feel bad," Conrad said patting Jack on the shoulder. "It's perfectly normal. It's an emotional time and it's been a long time ago."

"Maybe when you talk to Leanne or Daniel, they'll remember something. I mean, they live there so they would notice little things I wouldn't."

"Maybe," Conrad said. "Well, I've got everything I need. Are you planning to go back to Mavis' tonight?"

"I hadn't thought, I don't know. They'll wonder if I don't, but…"

"Maybe it would be better if I got you a room in a hotel. I could drop you off there and we can work all this out tomorrow?"

"Why don't you just stay here, Jack?" Bryan said as he walked in the kitchen. "I've got a spare room and your car isn't here, so no one will come looking for you unless you said something when you left."

"Okay, I guess," Jack said looking between Bryan and Conrad. "Maybe I should call though or something. What if they start thinking I've disappeared?"

"Maybe a text would be better," Bryan suggested. "So, your voice doesn't sound nervous or anything. Just tell her we're going to watch the game or a movie, something that will make it real late and you don't want to wake up everybody coming home."

"Is Leanne working here tomorrow?" Conrad asked Bryan.

"Yeah, but she doesn't come over until 10:00."

"When does she take the kids to school?" Conrad asked Jack.

"I don't really know," Jack stammered.

"Okay, I think the text is a good idea, but after you send it, I still think you're better off at the inn. I'll talk to Daniel and Leanne first thing in the morning, but I'd rather you not interact with them any more than that until I do."

"Okay," Jack said taking out his phone and typing a text to Leanne.

"Can I trust you not to talk to anyone else tonight? That means Leanne, Daniel, Mavis or anybody else?" Conrad didn't want to lock him up although it was an option, but he didn't want Jack muddying the waters.

"Sure, Chief, but maybe we should just go over there tonight. I'm sure they'll tell you what they know."

"I'm trying to minimize the situation for you. I'd like the chance to try to get them to tell me the truth on their own. I'd rather do all that tomorrow."

"Okay," Jack said shrugging. "Maybe they'll listen to you."

"If they come clean tomorrow, they won't blame you. Let's try it my way."

CHAPTER 29

"Did everything go okay with Jack last night?" Cora asked Conrad when she answered his early morning call.

"I guess. I registered him at the Nutmeg Inn and told him to sit tight. I don't know if he'll do that or not. I'm sure he's itching to call Leanne."

"So, what's your plan today?"

"I'm sending a car out to tail Leanne to the school and pick her up after the kids are safely inside. I've got Tabor going out to Mavis' to pick up Daniel."

"So, you're bringing them both in?" Cora was worried about Mavis' reaction. "What are you telling them?"

"Just that I need a statement, need them to sign their statement and we'll have to see what that is first," Conrad said.

"Did you call Alice?"

"Yeah. She wants to have them charged, but I got her to agree to hold off today and let me see what they say. That's part of the reason I wanted to keep Jack away."

"Daniel might cave, but I don't know about Leanne," Cora said worried Leanne was going to make it worse for herself.

"I'm thinking the same thing, but this still doesn't solve the real question unless Daniel confesses to murder."

"You think he might have done it?" Cora said frowning. It was always possible if he and Howard argued, maybe things got out of hand. He was a strong young man.

"Not really," Conrad said. "But one of them might know who did. Covering it all up doesn't make sense otherwise."

"I still think Miriam is involved," Cora said. "I know you think she's all talk, but I think she can't handle her own rage. Maybe she didn't plan to, but I can see her getting angry enough to hurt someone. I've thought she was going to hurt me before."

"There are still angles I haven't explored," Conrad said. "Maybe it's none of them. I'll call you once I get through this and hopefully, we'll know something more."

§

"Sorry to bring you in, Daniel," Conrad said as he sat in the chair across from Daniel in the interview room. "I've just got limited time today to see a number of people and I couldn't get out of the office."

"That's okay," Daniel said with his hands under the table.

"Now, I know we talked yesterday, but I think you left some parts out and I want to make sure I get it all down when we complete your statement." Daniel stared at a point in the middle of the table and said nothing. "Okay, let's start at the beginning of your day, that last day you saw Howard. It was December 17, 1999. Correct?"

"Yeah," Daniel said and raised his head slightly.

"So, tell me what you did. You woke up and…"

"I don't remember. I guess it was like any other day."

"Okay, what do you do any other day?" Conrad suddenly flashed back to his last conversation with Daniel. He had forgotten how painfully slow it had gone.

"Got up, got dressed, ate breakfast, went to school," Daniel smirked at Conrad and looked him in the eye.

"So, did you eat with Howard?"

"No."

"Who did you eat breakfast with?"

"I just got myself some cereal. We just ate whenever we wanted."

"Okay, where was Howard?"

"I don't know. I guess in the living room. He usually sat in front of the TV in the morning and watched the news."

"Okay, what time did you leave for school?"

"I think it was like 7:40 when the bus came by."

"Did Leanne ride the bus, too?"

"Sometimes," Daniel said shrugging.

"Just a minute. I'll be right back," Conrad said and left the room.

§

"Tabor, where did you put her?"

"Oh, hey Chief. She's in Interview Room Four."

Conrad opened the door and Leanne glared at him angrily. "I'm sorry for bringing you in here, but I'm really strapped for time today and I couldn't run back out to the nursery. I hope you don't mind."

"You could have just called me. I'd have come in."

"Well, I didn't think you were home. I thought you had to take the kids to school, so I had the officer intercept you, so you didn't drive to town twice."

"Okay," Leanne said with a huff. "I'm here.

What do you need?"

"First, can you come back out to dispatch with me. I need some basic information and then I'll be able to finish up."

"Sure," Leanne said standing and following Conrad out into the foyer.

As soon as they were in front of Interview Room Two, Conrad stopped. "Wait here just a minute for me. I've got to get something from my office."

"Okay," Leanne said as she stood idly looking around and spotted Daniel through a window in Interview Room Two.

Conrad looked around his office for a report form he could use and gave the siblings ample time to see each other.

"Okay, I got it. Let's go in this first room. It's empty now." Conrad waited until Leanne was seated and gave her a statement sheet. "If you can fill out the demographic information on the top, that will get us started and I'll be right back."

§

"Okay, sorry for that. Let's get back to where we were. You rode the bus to school that day, but you don't remember if Leanne did or not. Is that correct?"

"Yeah. I mean she usually did, but I don't remember that specific morning."

"Right. Right. It was just a normal day for you," Conrad said crossing one ankle over his knee and pretending to write on the pad of paper he brought back in with him.

"Did you stay at school all day?"

"Yeah."

"You seem certain of that."

"I am," Daniel said sneering. "You think I left school and went home and killed Howard?"

"Not unless you had a friend with a car," Conrad said.

Daniel huffed. "Look, I don't know anything. We've already talked about that."

"Yes, and I have to say, that is what troubles me the most," Conrad said putting his leg down and leaning forward on his elbows. "I know that's not true and I can't figure out why you'd lie about that unless you're covering up something even bigger."

"I don't know what you're talking about."

"Who do you think killed Howard?"

"I don't know," Daniel said throwing his hands out at his sides.

"Do you think Leanne and Jack came home in the middle of the day and did it? Maybe it was your mom?"

"What? No! None of that is true," Daniel yelled.

"So, why are you keeping secrets? If it's not for your mom or your sister, who are you trying to protect?"

"I don't know what you're talking about," Daniel said again leaning back in his chair and lowering his head.

"I think you do, and I know you'd feel a lot better about things if you'd get that secret off your chest. I mean, it's not really a secret anymore. I know and, well, everybody in this station knows, so it isn't your secret anymore."

Daniel stared down at the edge of the table without speaking.

"You think about it. I'll be back." Conrad left the room quickly and went into Interview Room One.

§

Conrad rushed into Leanne's room, turned the chair backwards and straddled it. "Sorry," he said breathlessly. "Let's get back to this now."

"Okay, I filled in the top. What do you want me to put in the bottom part?"

"I wanted to ask you something, something I forgot when we talked before," Conrad said.

"Sure."

"Did you ride the bus to school that day? The day Howard died?"

"Probably. I mean I usually did because Jack went to school early. I don't really remember the morning specifically."

"Did you and Jack stay at school all day? I mean did you ever cut classes or leave campus for any reason?"

"No, we were there all day."

"What about Daniel? Do you know if he was at the school all day?"

"I can't say for certain. I mean I just saw him in passing, but I'm sure he probably was. He rode the bus home."

"How do you know he did?"

"Well, I guess I don't. He was almost always home before I was. How else would he get there?"

"I don't know," Conrad said shrugging. "He was sixteen, wasn't he? I mean I'm sure he had friends who had cars at school."

"Maybe," Leanne said shrugging. "Why don't you ask him?"

"Oh, I have. I just wanted to see if you knew."

"He was my kid brother. I didn't pay a lot of attention to him or his friends back then."

"Oh, okay. So, tell me about when you got home. Jack brought you home, right?"

"Yeah, he usually did unless he had to stay after for something."

"So, start there," Conrad said picking up his pad of paper and holding his pen as if he was ready to write.

"Jack brought me home from school," Leanne said slowly. "Daniel was already there. That's all there was."

"Daniel was inside the house?"

"No, he was out on the porch," Leanne said and then added, "I think".

"You and Jack got out of the car and walked up,"

Conrad said nodding, "and what did Daniel say?"

Leanne frowned. "Hi, I guess. I don't remember."

Conrad shook his head in disappointment. "Oh, come on. You remember, don't you?"

"No," Leanne said indignantly. "Why would I remember something like that? It was just a regular day. Nothing special."

"Wow, really?" Conrad said. "I mean I've never buried my stepdad, but I'd think that would be a little memorable."

"What? I didn't bury anybody," Leanne yelled as she jumped to her feet.

"That's true, I guess," Conrad said leaning back and shrugging his shoulders. "You just told your brother to do it. Does everybody do what you tell them to? It must be a tremendous feeling to have that kind of power."

"I'm leaving," Leanne said stomping to the door and looking back at Conrad.

"You can leave if you want, but I'll have to arrest you then. I'd much rather see you cooperate and do the right thing. Actually," Conrad said pivoting in his chair. "I had hoped you would do that on your own, but it's obvious you can't tell the truth."

"I *am* telling the truth," Leanne demanded but stomped back to her chair to face Conrad.

"Let's just clear that part up right now," Conrad said resting on his elbows with a sigh. "I know you aren't, so you can stop wasting your time with that story. I know exactly what you came home to that day and what you did about it. Did you know it's illegal to disturb a dead body? It's also illegal when you fail to report a crime? Now you're failing to cooperate with an investigation. I've got quite a list to hold you on, so I'd recommend you think about this real hard and I'll come back," Conrad said standing. "Maybe it will go better the next time around. Sit tight."

CHAPTER 30

"Okay, Daniel," Conrad said pulling out the chair again to sit. "Let's start with when you walked in the house after school and found Howard in the living room."

Sitting there quietly, they listened to each other breathe for several seconds. "I know you're worried about getting someone else in trouble, but you're also impeding an investigation because you're withholding information. It only makes you look like you have something to hide."

"I was freaked out," Daniel said and then sighed as if he hadn't taken a breath in years. "I didn't know what to do."

"You didn't think to call the police?"

"No, I really didn't," Daniel said running his hands through his hair. "I couldn't think at all. I just ran outside and tried to breathe."

"That's where you were when Leanne and Jack

drove up?"

"Yeah, and I ran up to them and I told them. I told them I didn't know what to do."

"At this point you all three went in the house?"

"Yeah, Jack was going to call the police, but Leanne thought we'd get in trouble, so she stopped him."

"Why would you guys get in trouble?"

"I don't know. I guess she thought no one would believe we just found him."

"You didn't tell your mom?"

"No," Daniel said shaking his head in sadness. "I couldn't tell her. She kept waiting for him to come home and I just didn't know how to tell her."

"Have you and Leanne or Jack talked about this over the years? I mean as time went by and you got older, didn't you ever think you needed to tell?"

"Sure, I mean every time somebody mentioned Howard or mom said something, I wanted to tell, but..."

"Leanne told you not to?"

"Yeah, she said we could never tell. I told her mom wouldn't be mad. She needed to know. She even tried to find Howard, you know, online and things like that. She always thought he left her."

"Yes, I'm sure she was hurt by that," Conrad said. "So, what do you think happened while you were at school?"

"No idea. I mean, maybe he just died. He was old and he had stuff wrong with him. Maybe he just died."

"The coroner said he had a blow to his head."

"That could be just when he fell down, couldn't it?"

"I don't know," Conrad said. "I'm not a medical examiner, but they don't think so. It could have been an accident. Someone could have pushed him or hit him on the head with something. Maybe even thrown something at the back of his head. Did you see anything broken at the house? Or anything moved?"

"I don't think so. I mean I don't remember anything like that. There wasn't any blood or anything."

"You're sure? Nothing dried on the floor or carpet?"

"No, nothing. I just thought he died. I never thought anyone killed him."

"Well, you see," Conrad said. "There are a lot of medical conditions that can just kill you instantly while you're sitting in your favorite chair watching TV. I'm not a doctor, but I've been a policeman my whole life and I've seen a lot of things like that. He could have had a heart attack, an aneurysm, a stroke, an asthma attack, lots of different things, but without a body to autopsy, we'll never know if it was something like that."

Daniel looked down at his hands with teary eyes.

"Keeping this secret for Leanne has probably prevented us from ever knowing the truth, from your mom ever having that closure."

"I should have told mom," Daniel said sniffing

as Conrad saw tears drop onto his clasped hands.

"My advice to you, son, don't listen to your sister anymore."

Daniel nodded quietly.

"I'm going to leave you alone for a bit and you write down the details for me. Start with coming home from school and what you found. You'll need to explain the motorcycle and the sidecar, all the details, and I'll talk to the coroner for you. I'll be back shortly."

§

"Okay," Conrad said walking in calmly. He didn't really need Leanne's statement anymore. He was tired of the emotional roller coaster and thought it just easier to arrest her. "I don't see anything written on your statement."

"Is that what you need me to do? I'll write down what happened."

"Okay. You do that and I'll come back," Conrad said turning the chair back around and putting it under the table.

"If I come back and you haven't written down the truth, I'm going to arrest you."

"You can't just arrest me because I won't write what you want," Leanne said slamming her hand down.

"I'm not going to fight with you. I don't need you to tell me the truth. I already know it. I'm giving you this chance to save yourself. I've got too much to do today to waste it arguing with you."

"You might as well just lock me up then," Leanne hollered.

Conrad opened the interview room door and motioned for Officer Tabor. "Take her to holding for me."

"No!" Leanne screamed. "You can't do this."

Conrad just nodded and walked down the hall to his office ignoring the screams. Cora had warned him Leanne liked to make a scene.

§

Conrad shut his office door and poured some coffee in his cup. Pulling out his desk chair, he sat down to search online for a phone number to the local high school.

"Good morning. This is Chief Harris down at the PD. Can you access attendance records that are really old?"

"Morning, Chief. Well, it depends on how old. Is it before 2004?"

"Yes, are those older records gone?"

"No, they just aren't on the computer. You could call the school district office, and someone could pull the paper files, probably. They might still have them, but it would take a little while to find them."

"Okay, I'll try that. Thank you."

Conrad was fortunate enough to reach a helpful clerk at the district office who told him she would search the records for him and call back, so Conrad called Cora.

"Hey Connie," Cora said when she answered the call. "How are things going so far?"

"Well, Daniel gave a statement and he's all good."

"And Leanne? Did she make a scene?"

"Oh, yes," Conrad said chuckling. The release felt good. "You missed a great performance."

"Did you tell her you already knew?"

"It didn't matter. I just locked her up."

"Oooooh," Cora cooed. "You didn't."

"I did. I don't even think that will work though. The girl won't budge."

"Maybe she has more to lose or has more of the story than the guys do," Cora said.

"Does Miriam have any relationship with the kids?"

"I don't know," Cora said. "Not that I know of. I wouldn't think so since they aren't Howard's kids."

"If I didn't know better, I'd think Leanne was Miriam's daughter. They have a similar temperament."

Cora laughed. "Now, Leanne can be sweet."

"Yeah, when she's playing you," Conrad said.

"But Miriam can't pull off that persona at all."

"True," Conrad said as Cora chuckled again.

"Did you ever check on the attorney in Paxton Howard was using? Maybe he has something interesting to add."

"No, I didn't, but you're right. I need to see if that goes anywhere. I may have to talk to Miriam again though and I'm sure not looking forward to it."

"Well, you know I'd offer to do it for you, but since she just spits on me, I don't want to get involved this time."

Conrad leaned back in his chair and clutched his stomach in a hearty laugh. "I forgot about that." Years ago, Cora had gotten into a disagreement with Miriam at a Chamber of Commerce meeting and Miriam had spit at her when she had exhausted all of her scathing retorts. The Council had voted in favor of Cora's suggestion and Miriam had hated Cora ever since.

"I shan't soon forget," Cora said haughtily and then joined him in a chuckle. "Your next interview has got to be better than that."

"I sure hope so," Conrad said feeling the tensions of the morning ease.

§

"How is it going?" Conrad said as he walked back in Daniel's interview room. "Did you get it all down?"

289

"Yeah, I think so," Daniel said sliding the notepad over.

Conrad read through the brief but accurate retelling. It matched Jack's story pretty close. "Looks good. I appreciate you cooperating, Daniel."

"I'm sorry, Chief. I mean if I could do it all over again…"

"I understand, but you've done what you can to right things now and I think your mom will understand. I'd recommend you go home now and tell her. She needs to hear it from you."

"Okay," Daniel said standing up. "I think you're right. I'll do that."

§

"That seemed to go a bit better than the last one," Officer Tabor said grinning as they stood watching Daniel leave the PD.

"Yeah, if only they could all go that way," Conrad said. "Hey, will you call Mavis Bell and see if she can dig up Howard's attorney information? I'd like to give him a call."

"Sure, Chief. You want me to get the girl now?" Officer Tabor said as Conrad began walking away.

"No, let her sit a while longer."

"She's asking to make a call," Tabor said smirking. "Actually, she's demanding to make a call."

Conrad rolled his eyes. "Before you call Mavis, I need for you to run over to the Nutmeg Inn and pick up Jack Summers. You can bring him back and put him in an interview room. I've got a couple calls to make."

"Sure, Chief," Tabor said and headed down the hallway toward the side door.

"Message for you, Chief," Georgia called out from the dispatch office. Conrad took the message slip she held up in the air and thanked her as he turned to go back to his office.

Grabbing the phone, he punched in the number from the message slip and it was answered quickly.

"Hey, Jeanette. That was fast."

"Good news, Chief. I found all three of them. I wasn't sure we still had them, but your suspicions were right."

"They weren't there all day?"

"Two of them were, the boys," Jeanette from the School District office said. "Leanne was absent during fifth period and marked tardy in sixth period that day."

"Okay, thanks, Jeanette. You're the best."

Jeanette giggled. "Glad to help."

Conrad poured some coffee before sitting down. He couldn't seem to get more than a few sips out of each cup today and reached slowly for the phone again.

"Chamber of Commerce. This is Debbie. How can I help you?"

"Good morning, Debbie. This is Chief Harris and I need to speak with Miriam Landry."

"I'm so sorry, Chief, but Mrs. Landry isn't in today. Would you like me to tell her you called?"

"Yes, I would. I need Mrs. Landry to come down to the police station today before 2:00 this afternoon. If she hasn't arrived by that time, I will send an officer out to find her and bring her here. Please make sure she gets that message as soon as possible."

"Oh, okay, but uh, Chief, I don't know—"

"Thank you, Debbie." Conrad was certain that poor Debbie had been told to always give the same disappointing news to anyone trying to talk with Miriam. He wasn't wasting any more time with that.

Conrad heard a tap on the door.

"Jack Summers is in room four, Chief."

"Great. Thanks." Conrad looked sadly at his coffee and took one more drink before he abandoned it again.

CHAPTER 31

"Jack," Conrad said as he entered the room with his hand extended. "Did you have a restful night?"

"Not really, Chief," Jack said anxiously. "I mean the room was great, but I'm worried about what Leanne is going to do."

"Well, I'm not finished interviewing her yet. I suspect she'll be here most of the day, but I have talked to Daniel. That went really well, and he gave me the same story you did. I think he wanted to do the right thing, just like you have. He just wasn't making those decisions for himself. He's gone home now to tell Mavis and I'm sure she'll understand."

"Oh, I hope so. I'd hate for her to be mad. We really didn't mean to hurt her at all."

"I know. I wanted to ask you one more thing. That day at school, you said Leanne was there all day?"

"Yeah. We had a morning class together and ate lunch together. I brought her home after."

"Did you see her during the afternoon? I mean did you have lockers close together? Or run into each other in the hall?"

"Nah, I was at the other end of the building. I had shop in the afternoon anyway and it was in an outside building. We never saw each other until class was over."

"Did Leanne have keys to your car?"

"No, I only had the one set."

"But did she ever have your keys?"

"Sometimes she put them in her purse. I mean I didn't need them during the day. She still does that. Why?"

"She missed some classes that day and went somewhere. I just wondered how she left. If she went with someone else or if she used your car."

"I don't remember her saying anything about it that day, but I probably wouldn't remember. She did use my car sometimes to run to the gas station to buy cigarettes. She doesn't smoke anymore, but she did back then."

"Would you know about it? Would the car be parked in a different place or anything?"

"Sometimes. She'd always tell me when we walked out of school if she did. I didn't care."

"Okay," Conrad said standing and pushing the chair under the table. "I'll get somebody to run you back to Mavis' house. Daniel just left a short time ago so you may get there just after he's told her.

Maybe you can help her understand what happened."

"Okay, Chief. Thanks."

§

"Beagle and Toole, Attorneys at Law. Can I help you?"

"Good morning. This is Chief Conrad Harris of the Spicetown Police Department. I was calling to see if I could speak to Douglas Beagle regarding his client, Howard Bell."

"I'm sorry, but Mr. Beagle is in court today. Would you like to leave a message?"

"No," Conrad sighed. "I'm a little short on time. Maybe you can help me."

"I'm not at liberty to discuss another individual's case with you, Chief. I'm sorry."

"I'm not interested in the case file. Howard Bell is dead. We are trying to determine time of death and I know he was in regular contact with Mr. Beagle during the time in question. Can you look in the file and tell me when your office last had contact with Mr. Bell? Either by phone or visit?"

"I don't think I can give out that information. I'm sorry."

"Well," Conrad said. "I'll call the prosecuting attorney's office and have them subpoena that information if you'd rather, but I'd like to think your office would want to cooperate with the investigation into the death of their own client. Howard Bell has been dead for over eighteen years. There is no active case any longer."

"I'm happy to ask Mr. Beagle, but I can't do that without…"

"Where is Mr. Beagle right now?" Conrad shut his eyes and tried to calm his breathing.

"He's at the courthouse here in Paxton."

"Is there another attorney present in your office right now? Someone you can get permission from? Or do I need to send someone from the Sheriff's office down to the courtroom?"

"Please hold," the receptionist said before she cut the phone to elevator music and Conrad blew air out of his lungs.

Conrad heard a soft tap on his door. "Come in."

"Sorry, Chief," Georgia whispered.

"It's okay. I'm on hold. What's up?"

"Miriam Landry is here to see you," Georgia said with a sorrowful look.

"Put her in Interview Room Four and lock her in. I'll be there as soon as I get done with my call," Conrad said brusquely.

"Lock her in?"

"If you don't, she'll run off in five minutes. Trust me."

"Okay, Chief."

"Chief Harris, I'm Gordon Toole, an associate of Mr. Beagle. How can I help you?"

"Mr. Toole, I have a very simple question I'm

hoping you can help me with."

"I'm happy to assist the police if possible. What is it you need?"

"Mr. Beagle's client, Howard Bell, is deceased and we are trying to determine his time of death," Conrad began.

"Yes, I'm aware of the recent news events."

"Good. Well, I suspect he was in regular contact with Mr. Beagle around this time and I was hoping you had records that could tell me if there was any contact with your office on December 17th of 1999. I don't need to know details about his case or anything you feel would be a disclosure concern. I'm just trying to determine what time that day he died."

"I understand, Chief, and yes, we were anticipating your call. We did hear from Mr. Bell on December 17th. He left a message at 11:27am and Mr. Beagle called him back at approximately 12:10."

"Did Mr. Beagle speak with him when he called back?"

"Indeed, he did," Mr. Toole said.

"I'm delighted to hear that and that is very helpful. I appreciate your assistance."

"Certainly, Chief. We are very interested in the outcome of your investigation. We have long wondered about the disappearance of Mr. Bell. His case was at a very promising point in time and his disappearance was unexplainable."

"I have one other question and you may or may

not be able to answer this, but do you know if he reported to Mr. Beagle that Miriam Landry, his sister and partner in the LLC, had visited him that day? I have reason to believe she was there prior to his death and am hoping to confirm that."

"Yes, he did tell us Mrs. Landry visited that morning. He was calling to report just that. I don't know the details of that interaction, but I can confirm that much."

"That's all I need right now," Conrad said with satisfaction. "I appreciate this very much."

"You're very welcome, Chief. Good luck with your investigation."

"Thank you."

§

"Miriam!" Conrad exclaimed as he walked in the interview room. "It's wonderful to see you."

"What is so important that you felt the need to threaten the Chamber of Commerce to get me in here?"

"Threaten? Oh, no, there must be some misunderstanding," Conrad said earnestly. "I just left a message for you, but I am delighted they were able to reach you. I do have a few questions."

"What, Conrad? We've already talked about this twice. What more could you possibly need?"

"I need for you to tell me about December 17th, 1999," Conrad said as he pulled out the chair to sit across from Miriam. "Every little thing you remember. No detail is too small."

"How am I supposed to remember what happened on December 17th? I can't remember what I did last December 17th, and you want me to remember 1999? You're insane."

"Miriam, this is important, and I think that day is significant for you, too, so humor me. What do you remember?"

"Is that the day Howard died?" Miriam asked innocently and Conrad smirked. Miriam didn't do coy very well.

"Yes, Miriam. It is the day your brother died, and you may very well be the last person to have seen him, so it's important you tell me what you remember."

"I don't know when I saw Howard last. I have no idea where I was or what happened. This is ridiculous."

"Okay, well, maybe I can help you get started. It was a Friday and the weather was unusually warm that day. You and Howard were in a legal battle over the ownership of land tied up in your family's Stanton Bell, LLC. You went out to Howard's house to…" Conrad held out his hand for Miriam to take over.

"I will not sit here any longer," Miriam said jumping up from her chair. "If you are trying to dig around in my private life, you can talk to my attorney. I'll sue you for slander. You will not drag my name through the mud because you can't figure out what happened to my brother and I will not be accused of—"

"I'm not accusing you of anything, Miriam," Conrad said calmly. "I'm stating the facts. I want you to provide the details. How was Howard that day when you got there?"

"I did not go out to Howard's house on that day or any other," Miriam shouted.

"Now, we both know that's not true."

"I did not see Howard on December 17th," Miriam stated sternly. "Whoever told you that is lying."

"How do you know if you did or not? You said you couldn't remember," Conrad said and then chuckled at Miriam's enraged expression.

"Howard and I were not having a legal battle. I made him an offer involving some jointly owned property. I thought it best if we split it up because, clearly, we didn't get along well and owning something jointly with someone you don't speak to makes it difficult to manage the business at hand."

"I understand," Conrad nodded. "So, you made him this offer and he declined. Is that fair to say?"

"Yes, we hadn't reached a compromise yet." Miriam lowered herself back into her chair.

"Your legal matters are not my concern," Conrad said. "I need to know approximately what time you were there and in what manner you found him."

"Ugh, I don't know," Miriam huffed. "I assume it was most likely morning. I do all my business in the morning."

"Okay, so you showed up at his house unannounced and knocked on the door. How was he when he answered?"

"Just like always, I presume. I don't recall anything out of the ordinary. He was rude, but that was usually how he greeted me," Miriam said flicking her hand over her skirt to smooth a crease. "Are you concerned that he was sick?"

"Had you seen him ill? Or did he show signs of illness?"

"Nothing new," Miriam said. "He always had a dreadful cough but nothing else I noticed."

"How was he when you left?" Conrad asked with a lifted eyebrow.

"Well, I can tell you he was certainly *alive*!" Miriam screeched. "Are you accusing me of something here, Conrad Harris? Because if you are, I want an attorney."

§

"Mayor? The Chief's on the phone," Amanda called out from her office. "I'm heading out unless you need something."

"No, I'm fine. You have a nice evening," Cora said as Amanda waved from the doorway.

"Hey, Connie. How's it going?" Cora said when she picked up the phone.

"It's been a long day," Conrad said leaning back in his desk chair. "Do you have plans for after work?"

"No, not a one," Cora said. "Just going home and scrounge for dinner."

"I was wondering if you'd do me a favor."

"Certainly, if I can. What do you need?"

"Well, I'd like to have Mavis up here when I interview Leanne for a final round, but I don't really want to send someone out there in a squad car to fetch her. Daniel went home today to tell her what happened and Jack's there. I'm sure it's been a really rough day for her. I thought maybe if you went out and brought her back, it might go over easier on her. Do you mind?"

"I don't mind at all. I'm happy to do it."

"Thank you."

"Do you think Leanne is ready to be honest with you now?" Cora said clicking her computer to shut down for the day.

"She's been in holding for about four hours. I did go talk to her about an hour ago and explained to her how it is. If she's not ready now, she's never going to be."

"Well, you know, if this had been back in 1999, I'd say she'd never crack. She was stubborn and strong-willed back then. Now, she is softer. She's a mom and she loves her kids. Still hot-headed and prone to outbursts, but she has matured, and she isn't as selfish as she once was. I think you have a shot at it now."

"Was that a vote of confidence?" Conrad chuckled.

"It's not a statement of your interviewing skill at all. It's just an observation of her personality. She's not easily manipulated. That might be an ugly word, but it is in essence what you're trying to do."

"Yeah, I'd rather not call it that," Conrad said scowling.

"I'm just suggesting you might have more success using her kids as leverage. I'm sure she doesn't want to let them down. Have you talked to Alice about this?"

"I did, but nothing too specific yet. Of course, she wants it referred to the prosecuting attorney, no exceptions, but that's on standby for the time being."

"I don't think Mavis will be surprised by anything that comes out of this now that she's heard Daniel's story," Cora said pulling her purse from her desk drawer. "I'm on my way out now. I'll be there shortly."

§

Conrad sat in the interview room waiting for Leanne to be brought up from the holding cell. Regardless of the outcome of this interview, she would be transported to the county jail in Paxton tonight. The coroner had already advised him the prosecutor determined there was enough evidence to hold her. How she handled things from this point forward would make all the difference.

When the door opened, a very different young woman walked in. Leanne Summers looked tired and her anger had simmered to loathing. She sneered at Conrad as she sat down across from him.

"Leanne, before we begin, I want to tell you that our conversation is being recorded," Conrad said as he pointed to the camera in the corner of the room. "I understand you have been read your Miranda rights and have not chosen to have an attorney present at this time. Is that correct?"

"Yeah."

"Let me begin by telling you the events of December 17, 1999, have all been disclosed by others involved. Your personal interactions with your stepfather that afternoon are what we still need to discuss. The events that took place after school are not in question."

Leanne did not acknowledge Conrad's words but kept her head down as she stared at the cuffs around her wrists.

"I'm hoping you are ready to make a statement and explain to me what happened when you went home in the middle of the day."

Leanne looked at Conrad and then at the camera but didn't speak.

"I've asked your mom to come up to the station so you can see her. She should be here shortly. Jack and Daniel are at home with your girls. I don't know if the children know yet, but you will be transported to the county jail tonight so you might want to talk to your mom about what you'd like her to tell the girls."

Leanne raised her chin up and her eyes were laced with panic. "Why do I have to go to the county jail? I didn't do anything to Howard. I didn't kill him."

"Why don't you tell me what happened when you went home after lunch that day?"

"I just wanted to talk to him. He was trying to keep me and Jack apart and every time I tried to talk to him, somebody got in the middle of it. Mom didn't want us to fight and she would interrupt. I needed some way to just talk to him and explain."

"Okay," Conrad said nodding. "So, you left school and went home to talk to Howard. What happened when you walked in?"

"He was sitting in the chair in the living room and he yelled at me wanting to know why I wasn't in school. I told him I came home to talk to him."

"Was he receptive to that?"

"No, he said there was nothing to talk about. He'd already made up his mind I wasn't going with Jack after graduation and that was final."

"What was the urgency?" Conrad said frowning. "Why were you two discussing this when graduation was months away?"

"Because he wanted me to enroll and take the entry exam at the Tech School in Paxton, which was in January. I told him I wasn't going to stay here after graduation. I was going with Jack. He said I wasn't."

"Did you feel like he would prevent you from leaving?"

"He said he would, and Jack was afraid of him. I thought I could reason with him."

"Okay," Conrad said leaning back. "So, Howard said there was nothing to talk about and then you gave him your side of the story?"

"Yes, I explained what I planned to do. I knew what I wanted to do with my life and there wasn't anything he could do about it."

"Was this a calm discussion?"

"No. He was yelling at me and I was yelling back," Leanne said as she dropped her head. "He was coughing really hard. He was mad and all the yelling was making him cough more."

"Howard had asthma," Conrad said as Leanne raised her head again and looked him in the eye.

"I took his inhaler," Leanne said softly. "He was asking for it and I had it in my hand."

Conrad didn't say anything. He let her cry.

§

"I'm so hungry, I can't even think. Bring me whatever you have already cooked, Jo," Conrad said as he slid in a booth at the Ole Thyme Italian

Restaurant. "I think I forgot to eat lunch!"

"Oh, no," Joanne giggled as she handed them both menus and Cora rolled her eyes.

"I'm pretty hungry myself," Cora said sliding in the other side of the booth. "Emotionally drained as well. You must be exhausted."

"Yeah, but I think it ended as well as it could," Conrad said as Joanne returned with drinks.

"If you're looking for hot and quick, Chief," Jo said pulling out her pad, "we've got lasagna on special tonight."

"Sounds great. I'll take that," Conrad said settling into his seat.

"I'll do that as well," Cora said handing back the menu as Joanne scurried off to get their order.

"So, you think they'll let her off?" Cora's brow was creased with concern.

"I can't say for sure. I'm assuming they'll want to charge her with involuntary manslaughter, but they have nothing to support the inhaler story unless she pleads. I don't think she'll do that."

"If she gets a decent lawyer, I'm sure they'll see to that. Mavis plans to do that tomorrow."

"Her biggest worry should be Miriam. If she sees a way to make money, she'll want to file a wrongful death case. Whatever Mavis and the kids are due on the land heist, Miriam will take back in compensation. She'll find a way to keep that land.

"Mavis has really been through it today. I can't imagine finding all this out eighteen years later. I don't have kids so maybe I don't understand, but

I'd think it would be hard to accept knowing they did all that and kept it from me all these years." Conrad leaned forward with his elbows on the table. "I have to say though, I think Leanne's tears were real."

"I'm glad they were."

ⓞⓞⓞⓞⓞⓞ

★ The Spicetown Star ★

~ OBITUARIES ~

--- Howard Anderson Bell, 51, of Spicetown, Ohio, died Friday, December 17, 1999.

He was born in Spicetown, March 12, 1948, the son of the late Erwin and Nora Stanton Bell of Spicetown and was a resident of the area all of his life.

Howard Bell was previously employed at Paxton Mine No. 9 until the mine was closed November of 1999 following an accident that fatally injured two miners.

He is survived by his wife, Mavis Bell of Spicetown and two siblings, Miriam Bell Landry of Spicetown and Wanda Bell Vaughn of Alpharetta, Georgia.

Funeral Services will be held Thursday at 11:00am in the Coley Funeral Home. Interment will be in the Fraser Cemetery on Rosemary Road.

Friends may call at the funeral home Wednesday from 7 to 9pm.

TODAY 62 37 TOMORROW 58 41

STOTLAR NURSERY
Your Garden
HEADQUARTERS

Sheri Richey

Next in The Spicetown Mystery Series

Spilling the Spice

I'd love to hear from you!

Find me on Facebook, Goodreads, Twitter, my website or join my email list for upcoming news!

www.SheriRichey.com

Made in United States
Orlando, FL
09 December 2022

25725085R00189